(DCI Lan

C000023589

THE KIDNAPPER'S WORD

BY

E.J. WOOD

Black Cat Books

The Kidnapper's Word by E.J. Wood

1st edition

'One missing child is one too many.'

John Walsh

~

'The Boogeyman doesn't exist, Emily.'

PROLOGUE

"Deadly emotions, buried alive, never die"
Joyce Meyer

Why "six feet under"? It was a common euphemism, and I've always wondered about the origin. That was until I was told that it all started with the plague. It came from an outbreak back in 1665, and as the disease swept throughout England, the Mayor literally laid down the law about how to deal with the ever mounting corpses to avoid further contagion. In the "Orders Conceived and Published by the Lord Mayor and Aldermen of the City of London Concerning the Infection of the Plague", he stated, "All graves shall be at least six feet deep". I wasn't entirely sure of the truth of the matter, especially as modern American laws only required a minimum of 18 inches of soil, but I'm almost positively sure that was only a buffer between a casket and the top layer – so any chance of a body rising to the surface was little if any. I had to keep digging, I didn't have a coffin. I wouldn't want the bones of the dearly departed inconveniently resurfacing; there had to be a minimum depth to keep the dead down where they belonged, and I certainly didn't want this body found because of poor burial. That would seriously affect the outcome I'm after. No, I can't take that chance. I needed to take the time and the care to ensure it was done right.

Burying the departed seemed apt. After all, people have lived in and around London for the last 5,000 years, and the dead were buried in large numbers under what is now considered a popular tourist attraction – the capital of Britain, London, or Londinium, as it was known back in Roman times. Although during the early history of the Roman conquest of Britain, people were also interred without coffins and left to decompose so they could reuse the grave. I'd rather this one stayed put because some things are best left buried.

The irony that Sussex played a key role in the Roman conquest of Britain with some of the earliest signs of Roman presence in this very county amused me. I couldn't think of a more fitting ending.

Time was ticking on. I looked up towards the darkening sky. I'd been out here for two hours already, but then I had all night to complete the task at hand. I wiped the sweat from my forehead with my forearm and breathed in deeply the crisp damp air, and after two hours of huffing and puffing, I stopped. That should do it. I nod as I slam the shovel into the ground beside the dirt mound so I can haul myself out. After all, this area was well above the water table so there was no chance of flooding from the heavy rains.

I looked across at the body; the lifeless corpse that lay on the ground. It was a moving experience to see a human being transition to a cadaver. Seeing it makes it real. I guess that would explain the need for open caskets. It lay there in the half light, motionless as if admiring the night sky. The skin was greying with lack of a pink hue in the cheeks, and the blood was tangled in the hair. I expected to cry, yet the truth was I felt nothing. I felt during this moment in time I would never feel anything ever again.

I wondered and analysed the best way to place it into the grave before wrapping my hands around the ankles; but I paused wondering if the skin was cold. I put my gardening gloves back on to save myself the shock of what might be. I grabbed the ankles and took a deep breath.

'Okey dokey then…here we go. Dead weight? No kidding. One...two...three...' I huffed as I heaved the body into the hole and began shovelling heaps of dirt on top.

As the darkness of the night sky crept in, it came with a promise of starlight. A time I could reflect upon the day's events, but the movement of shadows held me frozen like a fox in the headlights. I could hear my pulse beating in my ears as terror was sucked from every breath I exhaled, but I couldn't scream because I wasn't meant to be here. With the lucid moon I kept shovelling, you see, the one thing about new beginnings is that they require something else to end.

CHAPTER 1

You are cordially invited to …

Ava was never a big drinker. She liked a glass of wine or two, but she never considered herself an alcoholic – far from it. She could take it or leave it, but Claudia Henderson had been topping up Ava's glass since she arrived two hours ago. Ava had meant to keep an eye on her alcohol intake, but she didn't know how else to cope with the most recent disastrous chapter in her life.

'Ava, don't cry. He's not worth it.' Claudia smiled whilst pouring more wine into Ava's empty glass.

'You don't understand,' Ava choked on her words, wiping her tears away from her eyes.

'Is that why he couldn't make it tonight?' Claudia asked whilst stroking Ava's shoulder. Ava wasn't raised to make a scene to become the centre of attention, but drowning her sorrows had seemed like a good idea at the time. She was angry but frustrated at how to deal with it without looking needy and pathetic. Everyone was a little tipsy, so Ava seethed, quietly snorting her runny nose, and frequently sipped her never ending wine supply.

'Who's ready for main?' Claudia asked as she stood up cupping her hands together. Claudia and her husband, Wallace, were newcomers to the area, and once Claudia fixed her eyes on Ava there was no escaping her clutches. Claudia was the type of woman every man wanted, but every woman wanted to be. She was the most astonishing woman Ava had ever laid eyes on, and her face looked like it had been cut right out of a Playboy magazine. Something radiated from her that made her irresistible to both genders, and even at forty-two years old, she had that billboard complexion. Age couldn't touch this kind of beauty, it was just there. Ava was almost thankful that her boyfriend, Detective Chief Inspector Clarence Landon, couldn't make it.

Ava excused herself to the bathroom before Claudia served the main meal. She looked into the mirror at her seemingly normal face looking back at her and observed her red puffy eyes. She swallowed deeply and tucked stray dark hairs behind her ears before lifting the toilet seat. As she sat trying to calm her breathing, a knock pounded on the door. She jumped, holding her breath before answering.

'Just a minute!'

'You all right in there, Ava?' a concerned Wallace called out.

'Yes, I'll be right out. I just had a little too much to drink.'

'All right, dear. I'll keep your seat warm.'

Ava flushed the toilet, grabbed her glass, and walked back into the dining room.

Wallace was the new neighbourhood tits-pervert, and before Ava re-seated herself at the dining table, she took another gulp of wine. She wished Clarence was here, after all.

She smiled broadly as she walked towards her hosts. The Hendersons certainly made their home very attractive. The dining room was a beautiful grand space with a huge, rectangular mahogany table that took up most of the room. The other two guests, whom Ava had never met, were seated quietly with their hands in their laps; they didn't dare place their unworthy fingerprints onto the perfectly varnished table. Wallace sat at the head and gestured for Ava to sit beside him, of course.

Wallace was the definition of tits-pervert: someone who unsuccessfully attempted to join in private discussions between female comrades. It almost always resulted in verbal aggression on his part and caused irritating behaviour whilst he attempted to gain the attention of said females by offering unwanted drinks despite constant knock-backs. The usual tell-tale signs of a tits-pervert may be a receding hairline, beer-gut, corny chat-up lines, never realising that the women he is chatting up are indeed young enough to be his daughters.

'Ava! Come and sit here.' Wallace patted the chair as he smiled towards her. She half expected him to lean over and ask if he could ogle at her mammaries.

'This looks delicious, Claudia, thank you,' Ava whispered.

'The pleasure is all ours, Ava. I believe you've met Jane and John from across the street?' Claudia answered in response.

'Not formally, but we've seen each other around.' Ava answered and smiled at the other couple who sat side by side, still with their hands in their laps. Both John and Jane gawped at Ava as they were eager to impress their hostess, Claudia, by showing an interest.

'Please, dig in. Anyone for a drink top up?' Claudia asked. Ava cupped her glass.

'I'm fine, thank you.'

'Where's this husband of yours? We've not even had the pleasure of meeting him yet,' Wallace asked.

'Oh, we're not married,' Ava answered.

'I do apologise. I just assumed,' he stuttered.

'No harm done.' Ava answered as she sipped more wine. It was the only way she was going to get through the interminable evening. The Hendersons just weren't Ava's type.

'So, where is he? It's nine o'clock, what could he be doing at this hour?'

'He's working the late shift.'

'I guess with all this assassination talk he's quite busy,' Wallace nodded.

'People aren't still talking about that, are they? It was in the US of A, and besides, that was a few years ago!' Ava retorted whilst rolling her eyes.

'Aha, and there I thought you were a quiet one, Ava. I will have you know John F. Kennedy was a firm favourite of mine. He will be sorely missed,' Wallace defended.

'Clarence will be back soon. It's the commute that kills it.' Ava responded just as the house phone rang.

'Please excuse me,' Wallace dabbed his mouth and walked away from the table towards the kitchen.

With Wallace away and Claudia engrossed in conversation with Jane and John, Ava put her hand in her pocket. She found a piece of paper purposely placed by Clarence; a message stating,

"My darling, Ava, I am an imbecile. But I'm afraid I had to work. You see, you are right, I do not need to measure footprints and collect the ash of cigars or eye up snapped branches. It is enough for me to sit and think, because I am the best. You see, every murderer is probably someone's friend, and if you are to be Detective Chief Inspector Clarence Landon, you must think of everything, and this is why I'm not there this evening."

Ava resisted the urge to smile and tried to focus on the conversation at the table, but all she could think about was getting home, checking in on Emily, and warming that bed up for Clarence. She stared blankly at the grandfather clock that ticked continually whilst she watched the pendulum sway back and forth.

'Ava's got a daughter.' Ava blinked and looked at Jane as she heard her name. Claudia beamed at Ava and lifted her hands.

'Where is she?' Claudia asked. Like she didn't know!

'She's at home asleep.'

'Oh,' Claudia sneered.

And there it was, the 'Oh'…

'I didn't realise she was invited,' Ava answered.

'Well….' Claudia started just as Wallace walked back into the room.

'Sorry about that, where were we? Ah…Ava...yes... Did I hear something about a daughter?' Wallace interrupted.

'Yes, mine,' Ava stated sternly.

'How old is she?' Wallace queried, rubbing his hands together.

'Nine.'

'A wonderful age,' Wallace smiled.

'It can be. I really must be going. Claudia, Wallace, thank you for your hospitality.' Ava stood up and tucked her chair underneath the table.

'Don't go yet, it's not that late. We haven't even started with Cluedo,' Claudia begged as she tugged on Ava's arm. She obviously wasn't ready to shut up shop just yet; it looked like Claudia's night had just begun.

'Perhaps when Clarence has some time off work we'll host next?' Ava assured.

As Wallace saw Ava out, he gave her a wry wink as he closed the door. She had only a few meters to walk before her lungs could fill a little deeper and her heart could beat a little slower. Ava lived alone with her daughter in the suburban cul-de-sac in the west side of Sussex, with Clarence staying over most nights. The commute back and forth to London meant over a two hour drive for him, but he didn't mind the journey now that he had a new car.

Every house pretty much resembled the next, each richly decorated with heavy curtains, flowery wallpaper, carpets and rugs, ornaments everywhere with well-made furniture. Plentiful paintings and plants adorned wide open wrap-around porches. The Henderson's home had been no different in layout; theirs had also been heated by a large open fireplace.

Ava steadied herself up the ornate railing to the front of her house and stopped dead in her tracks. Her mouth fell open. The door was ajar about four inches. Ava's eyes widened, and she pushed the door open and bounded up the stairs two at a time.

'EMILY? EMILY?'

CHAPTER 2

Gone

Ava's scream was nothing else than primal. She cried with more ferocity than any storm, and her hysteria fell thick and heavy as she frantically searched every room in the house.

'EMILY?' She shouted. Silence. The house was empty. Ava screamed like a banshee waking the sleeping neighbours whilst looking out of the window into the darkened street. She saw curtains twitching as neighbours peeked out from their homes to locate the source of the commotion, but no one came running. How could Emily not be here? Where would she have gone? Someone must have taken her, but who?

'Ava, is everything all right?' shouted a concerned neighbour.

'Clarence! I need Clarence! Emily is missing!' Ava screamed.

'Wait, what? I will ring the police!'

Ava sat motionless on the sofa; her breaths deep and heavy as she tried to hold back the tears. Not twenty minutes had gone by before sirens were heard outside. Ava was paralysed and rocked back and forth clutching the cushion, wide eyed and wild.

'Ms Willows?' the speakerphone asked. 'Please come outside.'

Ava stood, and once out in the open she sank to the ground landing hard on her knees on her porch. The cars' headlamps beamed at her like she was a common criminal. The neighbours stood outside on their porches with their hands covering their mouths, gossiping to each other.

Ava's sobbing was interrupted by her need to draw breath, and she stared at the ground as Clarence's car came to a screeching halt. He jumped from the car and ran to her aid.

'I came as quickly as I could. Where's Emily?' he asked breathlessly.

'I…I don't know,' she answered.

'You need to step over here. We'll search the house,' stated Atkinson.

'Atkinson,' Clarence nodded to the Inspector in an effort to take control of the situation.

'Guv'nor,' the Inspector replied, knowing he had undermined his superior.

'Landon, please,' Clarence corrected.

'Sorry, Detective Landon, I don't think that's a good idea,' Atkinson tentatively stated, knowing Landon wanted to go inside.

'This is my girlfriend's house, for Christ's sake,' Clarence answered despairingly.

'I know, but it's protocol.' Inspector Atkinson nodded and patted Clarence on the shoulder as the Inspector stepped inside the house.

'They're just going to check inside, Ava,' Clarence reassured her.

'Someone has taken her, Clarence,' Ava sobbed.

Ava sat in the passenger seat of the patrol car as she watched Clarence radio for backup. She knew how it looked. She left her daughter alone, and she was now Bad Mother of the Year.

Inspector Atkinson exited the house and confirmed Emily was missing. Ava's home was now officially a crime scene, and the neighbours were asked to go back inside their homes, but many still peeked from behind their curtains. The Hendersons were pretty tanked, and Claudia lifted her hand to wave at Ava and signalled for her to ring if she needed anything.

Clarence gave a description and a small photograph of Emily he had in his wallet to Inspector Atkinson as more detectives arrived at the property and dispersed both inside and outside of the house; each person wearing a nylon coverall.

'What are they looking for, Clarence?' Ava sobbed.

'Evidence.'

'Evidence of what? She's gone…oh my God…They're looking for blood?

Clarence sat beside Ava and put his arms around her. 'It's just protocol, Ava. We'll find her.' Ava blamed herself for Emily's disappearance. She rehashed her thoughts: what if Clarence wasn't called to work that evening, what if Emily had gone with her to the Henderson's, what if she just didn't go to the dinner party like she hadn't wanted to. That had been the subject of the argument just prior to Clarence leaving for work.

DCI Landon did his best to look stern, and as he calmed Ava, a woman walked her way alongside Inspector Atkinson. Clarence inflated his cheeks as he let out a long breath.

When DI Burke attended the scene, she signalled her equally ranking uniformed counterpart, Inspector Atkinson. He wore an open necked tunic with black braided collar and cuffs, a white shirt finished off with his rank badges on the epaulettes, and a Sam Browne leather belt with a snake clasp.

'Burke, long time, no see,' Clarence stated in heightened shock.

'Clarence, well what do you know! Good to see you again,' she answered, smiling and extending her hand. Ava looked at the hand and traced it to the face of a woman whose brunette locks fell effortlessly on her shoulders.

'Ava, DI Burke is here to take your statement.' Clarence smiled whilst shaking Burke's hand.

'This is DI Burke? Who you used to work with? Clarence, why can't you take my statement? You're a Detective,' Ava pleaded.

'I cannot because of my involvement with you; it's a conflict of interest. But I'll be here with you, don't worry.'

Detective Inspector Tenley Burke wasn't known for her tact. Clarence had previously worked alongside her for ten years and never knew her to work with compassion. She spoke with formal words of condolence as she listened, perhaps her eyes would flicker, but her hands and muscles were tense. To describe her expression would be like explaining a sheet of paper.

'Clarence.' DI Burke nodded as she sat in front of Ava introducing herself, again, as Detective Inspector Burke before leaning in close to ask the question.

'Do you know where Emily could be?'

Ava refrained from answering sarcastically. She knew Burke was there to help, and with the neighbours already sentencing Ava to a lifetime of bad mother-ness, now wasn't the time to make more enemies. She tried to think, and looked into her lap. Her eyes looked side to side as she tried to remember the last few hours.

'I….I was next door,' she sobbed.

'And you left Emily alone in the house?' DI Burke started writing down notes.

What an awful mother…

'Yes,' Ava answered.

'Have you been drinking, Ms Willows?'

'Clarence….' Ava looked at Clarence for help.

'It's all right, Ava. Just answer truthfully.'

'I had a couple of glasses of wine…' Ava said, 'but Emily was fine. I put her to bed around just after seven.'

'You're absolutely certain of the time?' Burke asked.

'Yes. I had…we had, Clarence and I had been invited round the Henderson's for 7 o'clock but Emily likes to watch this new show "Thunderbirds" at 6pm whilst she finishes dinner. It doesn't finish until 7 o'clock. By the time I washed up and put her to bed and got changed, it had just gone 7.'

'Aha…' Burke nodded and wrote more notes. Ava wondered if DI Burke believed anything she had to say. There was no reason why she wouldn't, but she felt the disdain in Burke's voice as she questioned her. Not having Emily in the house tortured Ava's soul. It was like every atom in her body ached with the uncertainty of Emily's well-being. She had gone from a wrecking ball to hanging by a thread; on the edge of imploding.

Clarence sat quietly stroking Ava's back. She could see him blaming himself for having to work the late shift, for not being there with Ava, the fight they had about wanting to be the perfect neighbours, and his encouraging Ava to, for once, let her hair down.

The phone rang and startled Ava, and her eyes widened with the urge to answer it. It could be Emily. It could be her kidnapper.

'WAIT,' DI Burke shouted as she put a tap on the phone before handing it to Ava.

'Hello?'

'Ava…my goodness is everything all right?' asked

the nervous voice on the other end.

Ava placed her hand over the microphone and mouthed to Clarence it was Claudia.

'Claudia, I've got to go. The police are here.'

'But…' Claudia squeezed in as Ava hung up the phone.

Ava could see the neighbours closing the curtains as they saw she was watching them; caught between the impulse to help and not to get involved. After all, this was a mother who left her daughter alone.

'So, Ava, do you remember how much you had to drink?'

'What relevance does this have? My daughter is missing. Shouldn't you be out there looking for her?'

'I need to see if your alcohol intake would affect the reliability of your story.'

'What?' Ava asked, exasperated.

Clarence stood up, 'Burke, can I have a quiet word…outside?'

After a few minutes Clarence walked back inside alone, and DI Burke had gone next door to corroborate Ava's timeline with the Henderson's.

'Ava…is there anything you need to tell me?' Clarence tilted his head to the side as his eyes squinted.

'No….what do you want me to say? I know I'm a terrible mother.'

'No…you're not. But are you sure you locked the front door?' Clarence asked.

'Yes…I think so…' but Ava wasn't sure. She placed her head into her hands and cried.

DI Burke observed the distraught couple. She had known DCI Clarence Landon for about ten years, and although Clarence teased her for being dim-witted at times they had remained good friends, clearly enjoying one another's company. She hadn't seen Landon for the last two years after their Superintendent separated them for a conflict of interest, but Burke always considered Landon a man of honour, honesty, and compassion but he never discussed his private life, and as far as Burke was concerned, Ava was just another witness. She checked her notes before heading towards the Henderson's.

The mother, Ava Willows is thought to have left her home between the hours of 19:15 and her return 22:25 and her daughter Emily Willows to have been taken also between these hours by a person unknown or known while the mother attended a neighbour's dinner party twenty-five meters from her home. Upon Ava's return, she found the door ajar four inches and the child missing. *Something was off.*

After corroborating Ava's story with the Henderson's, she proceeded to the upstairs portion of Ms Willows' home, accompanied by Inspector Atkinson.

'Anything?' Burke asked.

'Nothing! The house is clean,' Atkinson answered.

'See what the evidence team turns up. We should have the results in a few hours.'

'And the beat cops?' Inspector Atkinson asked.

'Tell the officers to be discreet,' DI Burke whispered.

'What's your hunch? Mother killed the daughter by accident by giving her too much sedative in the hopes she'd stay asleep while she swilled wine next door?' Atkinson stated.

'Let's not jump to conclusions just yet, Atkinson, but it might explain these.' DI Burke opened the bathroom cabinet and used her gloved hand to remove a plastic pill bottle with the label: Prescription for Ava Willows – Iproniazid.

'Iproniazid?'

'Iproniazid was designed to treat tuberculosis, but its most significant positive effect is that it has a mood-stimulating property,' Burke noted.

'I don't understand.'

'It is used as an antidepressant drug, panic disorders, that kind of thing. I know it was approved in '58, but because of the high incidence of hepatitis it was withdrawn in '61 and replaced with Phenelzine. I'll see if Clarence….DCI Landon knows about this,' Burke suggested. She placed the pill bottle into a plastic sleeve and continued searching the house. Did Ava do it? Did she hide the body and fake the child's abduction? DI Burke had seen far worse in her career, and she knew under the wrong circumstances people would do just about anything. She wasn't prepared to rule out any assumption at this point in time.

DI Burke called her co-worker as DCI Landon was forbidden to assist. The two officers, Burke and Atkinson, searched for the girl, and later all the neighbours were asked to also join in the search. A constable named Kirkwood was asked to search for Emily as he was only ten miles away at the time of Emily's disappearance. The initial search consisted of Emily's immediate family, including Clarence, and DI Burke, the constable, local law enforcement, and a privately owned German Shepherd also joined in. But although the search went into the early hours of the night, it ended without result.

Five days after the evidence team had scanned the house; Ms Willows was made a formal suspect with DI Burke citing that the evidence of withholding the presence of medication was the grounds of suspicion. It was a poor excuse to bring Ms Willows in; after all, she was the girl's mother, but whilst the facts of the case were insufficient to determine whether the girl had been abducted, the victim of an accident or voluntarily left home, it was all Burke had to go on and all she could do to be able to search the home without the mother present, even if it was just for a few hours.

CHAPTER 3

"A suspicious mind will see evidence of poison
wherever it looks".
Ian Gibson

The police station was a large, yellow-bricked
architectural building with a blue police lantern
hanging on the wall. It was next to the signage
"Metropolitan Police Station" that was above the
door. Outside were parked several models of the new
Ford Zephyr. The 1960s saw the emergence of the
new police car with state-of-the-art equipment, and
officers were given radios for the first time. Ava had
never been inside a police car before let alone a police
station and she jerked and panicked.

'Inspector Atkinson, get these handcuffs off Ms
Willows please.' DI Burke asked as she sat in front of
Ava at the station.

Ava jerked and winced as Inspector Atkinson un-
cuffed her wrists releasing the cold metal stabbing
that dug into her skin. She rubbed her wrists to lessen
the pain and looked around the room.

'Ms Willows, may I call you Ava?' DI Burke
asked.

'Yes.'

'I'm going to be recording our discussion. Could
you please state your name for the record.' DI Burke
asked frankly.

'Ms Ava Willows. What's going on?' Ava felt
coldness envelope her. Inspector Atkinson stood
quietly in the corner of the room with his hands
cupped in front of him like a statue.

'I'm here to interrogate you, Ava.'

'Interrogate? You think I stole my own child?' Ava sounded exacerbated. 'Where's Clarence?'

'DCI Clarence Landon is outside.'

'I want to speak to him,' Ava demanded.

'I'm afraid that cannot happen.'

'Why am I here? You should be looking for Emily.'

'We are...I can assure you, Ava, we are doing everything in our power to find your daughter.'

'I'm not involved in my daughter's disappearance! You're assuming I planned this.' Ava pleaded with the DI.

'Did you?'

'For heaven's sake... Why would I take my own daughter?'

'You tell me. What do you think happened here?'

'I think someone took Emily for god knows what and you're wasting time with me when you could be out there looking for her.'

'So, you think it was a crime of opportunity?' DI Burke asked.

'I don't know what to think, Burke.' Burke nodded and tried to understand from a mother's perspective. She hadn't spoken to DCI Landon about the pills yet, but that was next on her agenda. DI Burke wondered if thieves attempted a break-in and killed or abducted the daughter when she woke up. Scotland Yard was yet to rule anything out, including such a scenario. Although nothing had been taken – apart from Emily –, it was a more than plausible case that thieves acted in a panic, made a hurried mistake, and took the daughter. Metropolitan Police seemed to have a few locals in mind that fit the profile. Their backgrounds, mobility history, and current locations were all compatible with the time of Emily's disappearance. It seemed to fit the pattern of a man or men involved in a burglary gone wrong. But lack of evidence against the men in question caused the Met police to abandon charges against them.

Ava looked at the Detective blankly.

'I understand where you're coming from, Ava, I really do.' Burke tilted her head and tried another approach.

'Do you? Do you have children, Detective?'

It hit a nerve with Burke. She didn't have any children, and it wasn't through choice.

'No, no I don't, Ava.' Burke had to remember that Ava more than likely wanted to be cooperative and that the last thing she would want would be for suspicion to fall on her, if she were innocent. Sentimentality wasn't Burke's strong point.

'Then how could you possibly know what I'm going through?'

'I will find your daughter, Ava, one way or another.'

'You mean dead or alive?' Ava huffed.

'Did anyone know you were home alone this evening or going out without your daughter?'

'Only Clarence and our hosts, of course,' Ava answered quickly.

'Are there any other access points in the house? Do you use only the front door?' Burke asked more questions.

'We have a back door that leads out to the garden but it's rarely used. The front door is always locked.

'Do you have anything valuable inside the property that someone would know about?'

'Not that I'm aware of.' Ava shook her head.

DI Burke stood up and left the room. Ava didn't

know if that was a good sign or not. She seemed to be insinuating that Ava was somehow involved in Emily's disappearance. She knew from Clarence that when someone goes missing, suspicion immediately falls on the next of kin. She knew the burglary theory appeared absurd, and she had checked that house back and forth and not even her jewellery off her night-side table had been taken; it was in plain sight. Ava wanted to cry again. She heard about child abductions before, never thinking it would happen to her in their quiet neighbourhood; parents suffering for decades with uncertain anguish.

Ava gasped as she imagined Emily like the little boy that disappeared in the late 50s. A little boy, who was walking to his school bus stop alone for the first time, was lured by some stranger promising him a soda. He then strangled the boy and put his body out with the rubbish. Ava screamed.

'AVA?' DI Burke came running back into the room as Inspector Atkinson lunged towards the distraught woman. 'Did you remember something?'

'What if she's dead? What if she's like that poor boy whose body was thrown out in the rubbish in '59. I don't want Emily's face to be featured on milk cartons.'

DI Burke wrinkled her forehead. She knew what Ava was thinking about, the world famous case of a little boy from New York City, a case that went unsolved for years and made parents fear allowing their children outside unsupervised. The boy was never found, and ultimately legally declared dead. Clearly Ava blamed herself for Emily being missing.

'Get Clarence in here, Inspector Atkinson,' Burke demanded.

'Yes Ma'am.'

When Ava looked at Clarence, she saw his face was pale. She stood opening her arms and grasped him tightly whilst DI Burke looked at the photograph of Emily. She could see a clear resemblance to her mother even though the child had long blonde hair that tousled at the ends and bright blue eyes as clear as the sea itself.

'Ava,' Clarence looked into Ava's eyes whilst stroking her face, 'we will find Emily.'

She nodded in compliance. She had to believe Clarence would get Emily back. Together they would find what happened to Emily. If he didn't, she'd never forgive him, and he knew it.

DI Burke and Inspector Atkinson arrived at the Willows' property. They entered the girl's bedroom; a comic driven child's room where the walls were adorned with various posters of Superman; the girl's favourite superhero. The bed cover had been pulled back, like someone had just stepped out of bed, and a few drawers had been left open.

'What do you make of this, DI Burke?' Inspector Atkinson pointed towards the open drawers.

'Hmm... I'd have thought the mother would have closed these. The rest of the house seemed pretty neat. I'll ask Ava if she notices anything missing.'

The Hendersons stood outside on their porch watching the police officers traipse in and out of the Willows' house. Everyone knew that the likelihood of finding a child alive after 72 hours was slim. It was rare people went missing and stayed missing for more than 24 hours, and nearly three quarters of them were found within the first day. As time goes on, the chances of them returning home safe get slimmer particularly if they are vulnerable like a child or the elderly. Police knew the first 72 hours were crucial, but Clarence didn't want to tell Ava that, and they had seven years before declared dead in absentia. DI Burke took into account Emily's age, whether she had a history of mental health problems, and whether she had gone missing before. She delved into Ava's financial records, investigated whether she had been targeted for a specific reason such as owing a personal loan, as well as asking about her personal involvement with DCI Landon.

Would a nine year old want to run away? If she did, what would be her push factor? The things that might make her want to leave her home in the middle of the night. And what would be her pull factor, the things that might draw her to someone or something else, such as friends or another family member?

'What about Ava's car?' DI Burke asked Inspector Atkinson.

'Nothing; the Vauxhall Victor was clean. Only a few fibres on the rear seat, but nothing untoward.'

'Damn it,' DI Burke slammed her fist against the dresser.

Without a body or trace of a body they had no case and they'd have to let the mother go. Burke wondered if the child had gone missing earlier in the day or even the day before, but Landon's statement corroborated Ava's. They seemed like the perfect couple, but Emily clearly wasn't his daughter. They were hiding something. And she was yet to question other people that knew the couple. Of course at this point in time, DCI Landon was not a suspect. But, other than the mother, he was the last one to see Emily. Burke wondered if Ava had a babysitter – but dismissed it as the child was left alone. Did she have a cleaner? The house was immaculate after all. What was Ava's profession? Did she work? Would a colleague know she was alone this evening? The Henderson's statement seemed to corroborate Ava's as did Landon's, but could this just be careful planning on the mother's part?

Ava could have killed the daughter at any point between Landon leaving for work and the police arriving at the scene.

Burke made plans to visit the child's school in a few hours before the Missing People charity publicised the case by placing alerts and began dispersing posters of the girl at train stations and airports. If anything made a perp panic, it was knowing everyone knew what this child looked like.

CHAPTER 4

The first time I saw her…

DI Burke returned to the home of Ava and saw Clarence sitting beside her with his head lowered. It must be really hard on him, unable to help. His eyes were dull and unlike the shining windows to the soul they usually resembled when he is struck by a clever idea or revelation.

The term good cop or bad cop was merely an oversimplification of the real truth. Police officers can have a wide variety of attributes; some want to join the force because they're courageous and have a burning desire to help the helpless, others are devious and use their position for seeking their own kind of perverse justice in the world, and others are just normal people that get up, go to work and go home. But, given a change of circumstances any one of those attributes could rise to the surface. Landon sat motionless, like a ticking time bomb.

DI Burke stood in the corner of the room observing the couple. She was the epitome of authority with her sharp suit and her gun idly hanging in its over-the-chest shoulder holster slightly out of view. Ava wondered why she stood there, perhaps planning her next angle of attack.

'You don't need to look at me like that, Ava, I'm here to help.' DI Burke said.

'You could have fooled me,' Ava replied. 'Aren't you going to say anything, Clarence?'

Clarence lifted his head and turned it away from Ava. There was an awkward silence then Clarence asked Burke quietly, 'You're going to check out the school?'

'Yes, I want to see if there has been anyone paying special or unusual attention to Emily, but I have an appointment with the Head Mistress after hours. I don't want to alert any parents of a possible child abductor in the area.'

'Besides, the press will be all over this, I think we'd rather keep this quiet for now.' Clarence stated.

DI Burke was never one to deliver good news. She had the face of a mother, but she could never understand Ava's pain. She spoke of the law and the procedure and quickly changed her tone to reassure Ava that she was on her side. She thought how she could break the news with discretion, perhaps even with compassion. She had enough time to practice during her years in law enforcement, and as she watched and listened, her eyes flickered, her face muscles tensed, and she breathed deeply as she spoke of the delicate task ahead. In most child abduction cases, it is the parents who are behind it, and this case had been no different. Of course Burke wasn't about to rule out any other factors, especially as the step father had been a long term colleague of hers.

'Ava, Clarence, I can't imagine how difficult this is for you both…'

'No you can't,' Clarence snapped.

'But, do you have any idea who might have taken Emily? Has there been anyone new in your lives? Do you have any enemies, Clarence, who may have taken her as some kind of ransom?'

'We're police officers, Burke, we all have enemies.'

Ava's eyes started to well again with tears. 'Who would want to take our child? What could they possibly want with a nine year old child?' Ava said as she gasped.

'What? What is it, Ava?' Clarence asked.

'Do you think….no….please God no….' Ava shook her head. 'Do you think she was taken by a man for…?'

Burke interrupted Ava before she could finish, 'It's not uncommon for children to be abducted by paedophiles, Ms Willows, and I'm not ruling that out, but before we jump to any conclusions, have you come into any money lately that anyone would know about that may give reason to snatching Emily?'

'No…we just have our home,' Ava answered and looked at both Detective Inspector Burke and Clarence in confusion.

'And what is your form of income?' DI Burke noted.

'Clarence works and I do three shifts a week at the community centre. What has this got to do with Emily?'

'And where is Emily while you're working?' Burke continued.

'She stays with her friend Natasha across the road for sleepovers.'

'Aha…and how long has she done this?' DI Burke nodded her head.

'For about a year,' Ava crinkled her brows at Clarence.

DI Burke wanted to ask the question about Emily's father. DCI Landon never discussed his personal life, but Burke could tell by their relationship, he wasn't the one who had fathered Emily.

'Where is Emily's father?

Clarence's face portrayed his horror at the audacity of DI Burke and asked for a quiet word as Ava began to tremble.

'That was cold, Burke.' Clarence stated as he placed the kettle on the stove in the kitchen.

'Come on, Clarence, you know there is more to this than Ava is letting on.'

'All I can tell you is I am Emily's father, and that is all that anyone needs to know.' Clarence reached into the top cupboard to grab two mugs. 'You having one?'

Irritating to Burke, Clarence often concealed important details of an investigation, keeping Burke in the dark, and she knew this time was no different.

'Please,' she answered.

Clarence placed the three mugs onto the counter and unscrewed the tea jar as Burke stepped closer.

'But you're not, are you?'

'THAT'S NONE OF YOUR GOD DAMN BUSINESS!'

'Clarence!' Burke stepped away in shock.

'I'm sorry, that was uncalled for. I am Emily's father but no, I'm not her biological father.' Clarence was seething at the subject matter. He recalled the nights he would put Emily to bed and how she would tell him how she used to hear her mother and father fighting, how her mother would shout and scream before hearing loud thuds. Emily would push her face into her pillow to drown out the crying, and if one day "mummy" left, Emily wondered if she would take her?

'Do you know where he is now?' Burke asked tentatively.

'No, he's been out of the picture for as long as I have known Ava, and good riddance. He moved up north with his secretary.'

'How does Ava feel about that? Would he have

taken Emily? Does he need the money?'

'Ava doesn't discuss him, he never gave a flying toss about Emily, and he certainly doesn't need the money. I think he was some kind of contracts and claims surveyor, I'm not quite sure. I wouldn't go wasting time digging up that history, I'd have known if he was involved. When are you heading out to the school?'

'Tonight, I have an appointment with Mrs Arrowsmith at 20:00.'

'Here's your tea,' Clarence passed Burke her mug, and they walked back into the living room.

'Sorry about that, Ava, I'm just trying to follow up any loose ends. How did you and Detective Landon meet?'

For the first time since Emily's disappearance, Ava smiled. Ava filled every pause during her telling of how she and Clarence met with a deep breath and more conversation, and Clarence looked at her adoringly as she described the time they met. He laughed at her silly idiosyncrasies; things that made him fall in love with her but punished himself for a moment of happiness during this lurid time. He sipped his tea and as he looked to the side, he realised that maybe Burke was right, and he was blinded to the facts in front of him. Had his love for Ava obscured his vision? He had always prided himself on being a psychological detective, one that need not bother with the painstaking examination of physical evidence. Rather, he enquired into the nature of someone's character, whether a victim or a perpetrator, his underlying assumption was only certain crimes could be committed by a certain type of person.

As he took in the ambience of the moment

watching Ava describe how he walked into the community centre with donations and had set eyes on her for the first time, he felt a sudden rush. His eyes glimmered as he sipped the last dregs of tea and slammed the mug onto the coffee table.

'Are you having an affair?' Clarence blurted.

'Get out, GET OUT, JUST GET OUT!' Ava stood screaming at Clarence. She threw her mug across the room and yelled for him to leave the house. DI Burke took Clarence by the arm and walked out the front door as Ava fell to her knees in despair.

'What the fuck was that?' DI Burke asked exasperated.

'I can't do this...I can't just sit here and wait.'

'Why don't you come with me to the school before you do any more damage? But I do the talking?'

CHAPTER 5

"Theory helps us to bear the ignorance of fact."
George Santayana

Landon and Burke approached the school. Mrs Arrowsmith opened the door and immediately looked at Clarence.

'Clarence, I'm so sorry to hear about Emily,' she said.

'Mrs Arrowsmith?' DI Burke interrupted as she stretched her hand out for a handshake, 'My name is Detective Inspector Tenley Burke, and I'm the leading Detective on this case. DCI Landon cannot comment on the matter, he's just going to sit in, so if you could answer my questions it would be very much appreciated.' Burke was stern. But if Landon was going to be present, he needed to be seen and not heard.

'Certainly. Please, come inside.'

Mrs Arrowsmith sat behind her desk with her hands intertwined. She listened to DI Burke's questions, answered accordingly, and on occasion looked at Clarence with that *I'm so sorry* expression.

'Detective Inspector Burke, we have an enthusiastic, dedicated, and caring team of professionals here that ensure each child thrives on the many exciting opportunities we offer. All our staff are committed to making sure your child's experience at our school is a happy and successful one. We value the strong links we have with our families and warmly welcome visits to the school. In recent years we have been proud to receive national recognition and awards.'

'I don't doubt the school's capabilities, Mrs Arrowsmith. What I'm concerned about is protecting your students and making sure the school environment is safe for every child.'

'But Emily wasn't taken from school, DI Burke. I'm not sure I'm following?' Mrs Arrowsmith said.

Clarence sat up straight, 'She wants to know if some bloody bastard has been hanging around!'

'Clarence!' Burke scolded DCI Landon.

'I apologise. She wants to know if some bastard has been hanging around.' Clarence reiterated.

'No, that's quite all right. There was this one time…' Mrs Arrowsmith scratched her head; she felt awkward mentioning the incident and had dismissed it at the time. Did she feel guilt now having not reported it at the time?

'This isn't the time to hold back, Mrs Arrowsmith,' Burke urged her to continue.

'I was out in the playground around lunchtime a couple of weeks ago, and there was this man, which was a strange moment. He was apparently asking for wood, that's what the gardener told me.'

'And then?'

'He wasn't near any of the children. I didn't think anything of it. I asked the gardener only because I saw he'd stopped working.'

'What was he doing there?' Burke asked.

'Wanting wood. Here, I've got the report.' Mrs Arrowsmith retrieved a folder from the desk drawer and handed it over to DI Burke.

'This just says that a man was on the site of the school?'

'Correct,' Mrs Arrowsmith answered.

'No arrests were made?'

'Not that I'm aware of, Detective.'

'Can you describe this man? If he's a convicted sex offender, he will be subjected to strict licence conditions and will be liable to be returned to custody for breaching them. Can I keep this?' Burke put the folder aside and rested her car keys on top.

'Of course, anything I can do to help. I can't really remember what he looked like, if I'm honest. He was quite far away, but I must emphasise that at no point did any of our pupils come into contact with him nor was he invited onto the school grounds.'

'If we could speak to your gardener as soon as possible, it would be much appreciated.

The gardener was outside tidying up the last of his tools before he headed home. Burke and Landon caught him just in time. He corroborated the Head Mistress's story and also stated: "In line with their standard procedures, any uninvited individual would be asked to leave the outer perimeter of the school site which he did without delay". The gardener, however, did manage to provide the officers with a detailed description. The individual in question had been seen waving to children from his car. When the gardener approached and questioned his motives, the suspect explained how he was driving past, saw the wood pile and wondered if he could take some home for the fire. The witness described the man as having thinning, dark salt and pepper unkempt hair, estimated at about 5ft 10 inches tall, and between the ages of forty and fifty years.

'Let's get you home, Clarence,' Tenley stroked Clarence on the shoulder to offer reassurance. He looked at her hand and smiled.

'Don't,' he said as he took her hand off his

shoulder.

'Come on, Clarence, don't be like that.'

'I'm with Ava,' he said.

'Never stopped you before,' Tenley didn't take rejection well.

'A lot has changed in these last couple of years. If we're going to work together again, Burke, then I suggest you keep your mitts to yourself and stop being a jerk,' he snapped.

Emily Willows had disappeared; her mother left her sleeping whilst she dined next door – only realising Emily was missing around 22:30. Was she snatched to order? Intelligence suggested that a paedophile ring in Germany had made an order for a young girl a week before Emily went missing.

Could someone connected to this group have snapped a photograph of Emily at school, sent it to Germany, and upon the purchaser agreeing the girl was suitable, initiated the snatch? They have a strong structure that allows them to move humans from one country to another in a matter of hours, and it's frightening because it's so easy.

DI Burke drove Clarence home. They spoke very little the entire journey, the comforting incident hadn't played well with Clarence, and it put a question mark as to Burke's motives. One theory about Emily's disappearance postulated that it was a potential burglary gone wrong. Emily is said to have been abducted after waking up and witnessing the crime – but nothing had been taken. Scotland Yard hadn't by this point ruled this theory out as such a scenario would have the would-be burglars acting in a panic and not wanting to leave any evidence of their break-in behind.

Police identified locals who seemed to fit the profile. Their locations and backgrounds did at first seem to fit the burglary pattern, upon questioning by DI Burke, the police department released them based on lack of concrete evidence. Clarence never thought this was a valid hypothesis to begin with.

'This burglary theory, Burke, is absurd,' he said. One of the few things he said on the journey home. 'Not even any jewellery was taken, no money, nothing - just the child.'

'Then what's your take, a local paedophile?' Burke asked. The local area had been awash with perverts.

'There are currently forty-two people on the sex offenders register in the area. It's a magnet for perverts. You've got the school a couple of miles north, Castle Park ten minutes east, and The Wonders of Pirate's Cove at the Queensgate Shopping mall.' Landon answered.

'There have been a total of six sexual assaults in the area in the last two years with a similar modus operandi as Emily, where strangers had been spotted observing children at school.'

'I don't think this was a break-in. I think it's someone close, someone close....' he slowed.

'What is it?' Burke pulled over outside Ava's house, concerned when Clarence paused his train of thought and promptly changed the subject.

'Where have you been these last couple of years, Tenley?'

'Lately, I've been on the Susan Roberts case.'

'Operation Lawmaker?'

'You know about it?' Burke was taken aback.

'Of course, but I didn't know you were the lead Detective.'

'I'm not. I wasn't,' she answered disparagingly.

'If I'm not mistaken, the body of an unidentified female was found concealed in weeds off Watery Lane, near The Churchyard. The badly decomposed body was found by a farm worker.'

'All we know so far is that she stood at the side of the road, thumbing it, attempting to hitchhike...'

'I'm sorry what? Thumbing it?' The term "thumbing it" hadn't been part of Clarence's vocabulary.

'You know, with her thumb out. According to eye-witnesses, Susan was trying to get home. She had recently moved and wanted to retrieve the rest of her belongings. Whilst there, her friends claim she met a man in his early thirties, and the pair spent the weekend together before he dropped her off. She was seen by various witnesses at the beginning of the M1 headed northbound. We gather she managed to get a lift, a stroke of luck she must have thought at the time, but it appears her journey ended not half an hour from her desired destination. Her body was found in a thicket on a rural country lane.'

'What is the world coming to?' Clarence shook his head.

'She was naked and had been strangled to death.'

'Rape?'

'We believe so. The jacket found next to her body that she was wearing prior to her death, had been torn which indicated a struggle. We've got an identikit picture circulating; we're hoping it brings in a lead.'

Burke had been investigating two murders prior to her reencounter with DCI Landon. They bore a striking resemblance to each other: so much so that she believed they were killed by the same perpetrator.

The victims were both young females with their

whole lives ahead of them and were killed just eight months apart. Hitchhiking wasn't an unusual way of travelling, a common and normal way for young people to explore the country. Although it had never occurred for Burke to hitchhike, it certainly wasn't an unusual or worrying sight to see a woman at the side of the road. But then Susan Roberts' body had been found face-down in a thicket, sexually abused and strangled. It was abundantly clear she had fought ferociously against her assailant. DI Burke and colleagues so far had managed to piece together Susan's final hours by speaking to eyewitnesses who came forward following the newspapers' police appeal.

One man had spotted Susan getting into a saloon type car, whilst another reported that a woman, matching Susan's description, had been spotted at a service station later that same evening. Clarence remembered reading about the murders in the press; Detective Chief Inspector John McGuiness had given the following statement:

The Sussex Constabulary continually monitor these unsolved cases and will be exploring new lines of enquiry. I'd ask anyone who believes to have information in relation to the murder of Susan Roberts and Barbara Avenue to contact the team here at Sussex Constabulary. Thank you.

'So what brings you here, Burke?'
'DCI McGuiness reassigned me,' she replied.
'Now, that begs the question.'
'Of?' she queried.
'Nothing… I'll catch up with you tomorrow.'

CHAPTER 6

We all go a little mad sometimes.
Joseph Stefano

Ava quivered as Clarence came through the front door.

'Anything?' she begged.

Clarence shook his head side to side indicating he had no news and Ava sat rigid.

'We're going to have to talk to the press. Someone might have seen something or know something. We can't keep it hidden from them much longer and better to hear it from us,' Clarence said.

'Fine,' she answered.

'Good,' he patted her leg and paused.

'What now?' Ava asked.

'DI Burke found pills; your pills in the upstairs cabinet.'

'And?' she snapped.

'Are you depressed?' he asked.

'I don't use them often, I just….panic every now and then.' Ava looked ashamed to admit her dependence on the drug. 'Are you still trying to imply I had something to do with Emily's disappearance? Many mothers suffer from depression, it's not that uncommon,' she answered defensively.

'No, this is my own concern; you were drinking on the night in question.'

'Because I'll have you know those pills would have come in very handy whilst I was sitting at the Henderson's all on my *Clarence Jones*.'

'No need for sarcasm, Ava. I was only asking a

question. Why were you sitting on your own?' His brows furrowed.

'Claudia had too much to drink and was ranting to Jane and John next door about god knows what and I was…thinking about you, if you must know.'

'Where was her husband?' Clarence recoiled.

'Wallace? He was on a phone call.'

'Did you hear or see him on a call?' Clarence grabbed Ava by the shoulders as he asked her the question. Her eyes widened and they darted side-to-side as she desperately tried to remember that night.

'No….'

'I knew I had seen that guy before…the night of Emily's disappearance.'

'What guy? Clarence….what are you saying?' she begged. Ava's desperate plea hadn't changed Clarence's mind. He turned and headed for the front door.

Clarence slammed the front door shut. His eyes squinted, and then came his strut. The whites of his eyes turned black and his stare pierced the front of the Henderson's home. Jane peered from behind her curtain at the ruckus that was unfolding at the Willows' residence, and she saw Clarence storming towards the Henderson's.

'Eh, John, get a load of this. That guy, the copper just came out from Ava's house.'

'Shit, he looks like he's going to kill someone. Close the curtain, Jane, you'll give us a name, and all we need is to make enemies in such a close knit community.'

Ava reflected on what she and Clarence had just discussed, and her face fell as she watched Clarence storm towards the Henderson's residence. They had been so accommodating that now she felt tense. She backed away from the curtain, curling her fingers into a fist and radiated an anger she never felt before.

She opened the front door moments before Clarence climbed the Henderson's porch and yelled.

'CLARENCE!'

'GET BACK INSIDE, AVA.'

She stood horrified with her hand covering her mouth. Had fear brought Clarence to a rage? Did he seek to do harm? A biological function best left alone, but when we see something that frightens us, a part of us, a primal part of our brain is automatically activated to fight or flee. That kind of rage can ultimately destroy us. It can corrupt our way of thinking, our judgement, and impair our rationalisation, but Clarence was beyond saving now.

A man about five feet eleven inches, thinning, dark grey hair, and about forty-three years old answered the door.

'Mr Henderson?'Clarence asked breathlessly.

'Call me Wallace,' Wallace stretched out his hand. 'You must be Clarence? I saw you the other night,' he pointed next door to where he had seen Clarence before.

'Get inside.' Clarence demanded as he forced himself inside the Henderson's home with Wallace stumbling backwards.

'I'm so sorry to hear about your little girl,' Wallace stuttered.

'Don't you dare mention her!' Clarence grabbed Wallace by the collar and shoved him against the wall as Claudia came running downstairs screaming.

'It's all right, darling, go back to bed. It's just a misunderstanding, right, Clarence?' Wallace stuttered in panic.

Clarence looked across at a panic-stricken Claudia.

He lowered Wallace off the wall and shook Wallace's cardigan straight. As Claudia reluctantly walked back upstairs, Clarence pierced Wallace with a stare.

'Are you just going to stare at me, or are you here for a reason?' Wallace struggled.

'Enjoy itty-bitty-titties do you, Wallace?'

'I beg your pardon! I think you need to leave!' Wallace scoffed his words at Clarence's insinuation.

The following day, DI Burke was quite displeased with Clarence after reading that Mr Wallace Henderson had placed a restraining order on his neighbour. Clarence nodded in compliance with Burke's new restrictions. She sensed that Clarence and Ava's relationship had taken on a new level – the blame game, and she took that into consideration as she laid down the law. She understood they were under intense pressure, not just from each other but from the press, but Burke knew if there was something to find, she would find it.

'Look. I can't have you just going off half-cocked Clarence,' she said at the station.

'I know it was foolish.'

'Just because you're a certified shit kicker doesn't mean you can take the law into your own hands, Christ, Clarence! I shouldn't have to be reading you the riot act.' Burke was pissed. 'I could arrest you on an obstruction charge.'

'He has something to do with it. I know it. Ava said he left the table around nine to take a phone call, and he was gone several minutes. Let's go pick him up.'

'We're going to need a little bit more than that, Clarence, otherwise you'll just be pointing fingers at everyone.'

'I want a 24hr watch on him or I'll do it myself,' Clarence demanded.

'You so much as take even one tiny step towards his house, Clarence, and I'll be forced to throw your arse in jail.'

'Look… say my hunch is right. These types of bastards can't help themselves; sooner or later he'll make a move.'

Later that evening Ava divulged in more detail the events of that frightful night. She was concerned that Clarence was going to make a mess of the investigation by going half-cocked at Wallace. For her, the investigation was moving too slowly, and every day that passed she felt another stabbing sensation as she thought about her daughter. Ava was exhausted. She couldn't sleep and the house seemed empty and void of happiness.

'I can't understand. Why haven't they found any evidence of a trespasser, Clarence?' Ava asked Clarence helplessly.

'Because it was planned… Whoever did it was careful. Somebody didn't just stroll past and think, "Hey let's see what's inside". It was calculated, Ava.'

What was the norm for kidnapping a child? Was Ava to expect a phone call, a note? Surely she would have heard from someone by now if that was the case. Clarence explained there were no normal cases of child abduction. Ransom demands usually turn up hours or even days later, but generally if the child was taken for ransom they would have heard something by now. Besides it would be unlikely the perps would want to hang onto a child that long and risk being caught.

'Maybe we should offer a reward, Clarence?'

'And where do you suppose we get that kind of

money? That's not going to help – if they wanted money we would have heard something by now.'

Clarence stood up wanting to embrace Ava. He could feel the tension brewing and tried to grab her as she paced the room back and forth.

'You said you found out about my prescription from DI Burke? What if they think I've something to do with this? That I'm some kind of drug addict,' Ava worried as she bit her nails.

'So you've got some pills? Most of the country is on some kind of pill or another. If you have nothing to hide, then you have nothing to worry about.'

CHAPTER 7

One missing child is one too many.

Ava couldn't understand how she hadn't mentioned the fact before. All eyes were on her as she walked into the living room where Clarence and the Detective were sitting.

'Jenkins is missing, Clarence,' Ava wrinkled her brow.

'Who's Jenkins?' Burke asked.

'Jenkins is Emily's favourite teddy bear,' Clarence answered.

DI Burke was visibly annoyed, 'So do you need to change your statement? Clearly something other than your daughter is missing from the house.'

'Yes, I'm afraid so. I'm so sorry.' Ava hung her head down in shame and embarrassment, not wanting to admit even to herself that she had possibly hindered the investigation.

'Burke, Emily takes that bear with her everywhere, she cuddles it in bed,' Clarence stated.

'But a burglar wouldn't be interested in the child's welfare,' Burke retorted.

Ava ran upstairs as quickly as she could. Clarence and Detective Inspector Burke followed. Ava frantically pulled back the covers and opened every drawer in the room as she sobbed.

'He's definitely gone,' Ava crinkled her brows and looked towards Clarence for answers. 'Can't you do that fingerprinting thing, DI Burke?'

'They probably wore gloves, Ava. It was a cold evening.' Burke answered as she tried to explain the lack of evidence that supported an intruder had been in their home.

Burke looked at the couple who were now exhausted, frail, and desperate. She assured them she and her department were doing everything in their power to help find Emily, but Clarence appeared frustrated, unable to help with the investigation.

'But surely there must be something, what about footprints? They could work, right?' Ava begged.

Burke answered, 'Theoretically yes, every person's foot has a unique set of ridges that make up a print unmatched by any other human being, but it is highly doubtful the perp walked around your house barefooted, and considering all the other doors were locked from the inside with only the front door being ajar, it is probable that she either left on her own accord or someone encouraged her outside.'

DI Burke looked at Ava. She trusted Clarence but she didn't know Ava, and she wasn't sure how well Clarence knew her either. Burke had implied that with a lack of physical evidence or witnesses who would place a stranger at the scene that it had to have been one of them. Again, she trusted Clarence, and he had an alibi.

Burke withdrew the transparent bag from her briefcase and placed it onto the coffee table.

'Can you tell me about this?' Burke asked.

Clarence's eyes widened. 'Burke, I've already discussed this with you.'

'You've what?' Ava stood up and backed away from Clarence. 'You've been talking about me behind my back?'

'It's not like that, Ava,' Clarence pleaded. 'I told you Burke found them in the bathroom cabinet. It was going to be sooner or later she questioned you about them.'

Burke was horrified that Clarence compromised the investigation. Now Ava, if she had anything to hide, had now had time to fabricate a story to suit any hidden agenda she may have had.

'I suffer with bouts of depression,' Ava shamefully admitted.

'Can you give me the name of your doctor?' Burke waited with her pen in one hand ready to write down the name in her note book.

'Clarence?'

'Just give DI Burke his name,' he answered.

'Dr. Ken Hopper.'

'And his speciality?' Burke queried.

'The family GP,' Ava answered.

'Thank you,' Burke concluded. 'That will be it for now.'

As DI Burke was shown the door, Clarence gave her a look of consternation.

Clarence walked back into the living room and looked at his girlfriend. 'You need to tell me what's going on, Ava.'

'I've told you everything there is.'

'NO DAMNIT! Burke is onto something and I can't find out what it is. She won't share anymore information with me because I can obstruct the investigation. I can't help you if you don't tell me what the devil is going on.'

DI Burke walked out of the Willows' residence and stepped down off the porch onto the road. She glanced at the house next door; the Henderson's, where Mrs Henderson was peering out behind a curtain.

Clarence was a damn good cop and his hunches usually paid off, but without sufficient evidence he couldn't take Mr Henderson in. With Clarence, it wasn't, "all by the book". When his unit needed something done, he would just go off on some wild goose chase because of a hunch. If the Detective in charge was a stickler for procedure, he could have Clarence's badge and then go after his family, but somehow it never went down that way. Burke could imagine him being the kind of cop that would hand over some ominous brown envelope to a snitch whilst looking over his shoulder like a common criminal up to no good, while his gun and badge shimmered under some street lamp in the middle of the night as his trench coat blew open from a gust of wind.

Detective Inspector Tenley Burke felt like she had become the enemy. When Ava sharply stated, 'I thought you were trying to help us,' it went to the very marrow of her bones. Clarence had put his hand on Ava's as she answered Burke's questions as best as she could. Ava didn't really have an answer as to why she hadn't called a sitter. She just looked into her lap, ashamed of herself for being a bad mother. 'I just didn't think it was necessary to call a sitter at that time of the night for such a short period of time.' Ava had stated, shaking her head.

The Hendersons didn't have any children, and it wasn't the type of dinner party that catered for them either. Burke had a suspicious feeling they were swingers, and it accounted for the reason behind their disappointment about Clarence's absence on the night in question. Of course, this was just Burke's hunch.

Tenley and Clarence had never discussed their personal lives at work. Clarence always seemed content and level headed, but over the past few days DI Burke began to see cracks in their relationship, the relationship between him and Ava, and the longer the investigation took, the wider they would grow. Ava and Clarence's once united concrete stories started to show signs of cracking, and DI Burke could understand why; their daughter was missing and they looked for someone to blame with their nearest and dearest becoming the prime target.

Her next line of inquiry would take her to the office of Dr. Ken Hopper, the family doctor.

CHAPTER 8

Trust me, I'm a Doctor.

DI Burke left the Willows' residence and immediately rang Dr. Ken Hopper to make an appointment to corroborate Ava's story. Her car's engine sang as she headed north having managed to squeeze in an appointment within the hour. The roads were unusually empty, and she took the opportunity to reflect over her notes in her mind. Emily's mother and step-father, Ava and Clarence, say all they have ever wanted is to find their daughter, but the story so far just doesn't add up. No evidence suggested an intruder had even been in the house, no evidence even suggested anyone other than Ava or Clarence had even been upstairs, and the girl's teddy bear was missing. DI Burke was suspicious of Ava, and now there was a new person of interest, Dr. Ken Hopper.

As she pulled up at the Doctor's office and rang the doorbell, a smartly dressed man answered the door. He had a non threatening face like someone you would be happy approaching to ask for directions in the middle of the street. He wore a clean-cut suit and a loveable smile, and he moved slowly, deliberately, unhurried, almost choreographed.

'Well hello, you must be Detective Burke?' he said as he extended his hand.

'Detective Inspector Burke,' she corrected.

'Oh I beg your pardon. Please come in.' His voice was deep and southern and he spoke without the medical jargon that Burke dreaded. For the most part she understood, and he would periodically stop to allow her to ask the next question.

'I cannot believe she is gone,' the doctor said as he put his hands into his lap and fumbled his thumbs together. 'Ava must be distraught.'

'When was the last time you saw Ava?'

'On a professional basis?'

'What other basis would there be?'

'None, erm...,' the doctor scratched his head and stood to check his diary. 'Three weeks ago.'

'And what was it in regard to?'

'I'm sorry, Detective, but that would be breaching Doctor-patient confidentiality.'

'There's a missing child. Any evidence that could help us find her would be very much appreciated.' DI Burke exclaimed whilst trying to keep her calm.

'I cannot believe Ava left her alone in the house!' he shook his head. 'I should have known.' He shook his head disapprovingly. 'I hope you find the little girl.'

'I'm doing everything I can. I have the whole department out looking for her. What should you have known exactly? Why was Ava a patient of yours?'

'Ava was suffering from depression.'

'And... You prescribed her Iproniazid?' Burke noted his responses.

'Yes.'

'And when did you first prescribe her the drug?'

'About six months ago,' he answered.

'What was the reason you prescribed it to her?' she continued.

'She said she felt dead inside and how she would wake with a cold wash. She didn't want to get up in fact; she explained how she didn't want to move at all. It took all her strength to take a deep breath and crawl out from beneath the covers every morning.'

'Would you say she was or is suicidal?' Burke nodded whilst writing down his comments.

'Depression, DI Burke, often is the result of being bullied for a period of time that can be overlooked by friends and family. I tried with Ava to establish a positive mindset in a healthy and natural way rather than prescribe drugs, but she would often cancel her appointments, and thus medication seemed an easy alternative. With this alternative method of treatment we can take our patients out on walks, and we can bring so much happiness for a few moments in that day that would otherwise be swallowed up by menial tasks. I prayed the drugs would work, I couldn't bring myself to prescribe ECT.'

'ECT?' Burke queried.

'Electroconvulsive Therapy. It is a medical treatment most commonly used in patients with severe major depression or manic depression that has not responded to other treatments. It's a psychiatric treatment in which seizures in the brain are electrically induced in patients to provide relief from mental disorders.'

'Why do you think she stopped coming to your sessions?'

'Ava's life has a silent killer; depression. That kind of pain sometimes can be too much to cope with, even hard to deal with. I believe attending our sessions meant that she had to deal with it, and by not attending she could try to escape it, but it follows her around like a black cloud. It's on the inside eating her away.'

'But what can she be depressed about? She has a beautiful life, a beautiful young daughter, a loving partner.'

'She had a messy separation from her husband.'

'Did she talk much about him?' Burke's brows furrowed.

'Only that he was obsessively interested in gaining custody of their daughter. It wasn't a subject she felt comfortable discussing.'

'Perhaps the root of her depression?' Burke asked.

'I believe so,' he nodded.

With Tenley Burke out of Ava's house, Ava felt she could return to some sort of normality even though her daughter was still missing. She rearranged her furniture, putting everything back where it belonged after the evidence team had turned her house upside down, and she made Emily's bed, fluffing up her pillow. She pulled it close to her face to inhale her daughter's smell before placing it back down. She collected Emily's toys and closed the drawers like she did every morning, and with the house so quiet, Ava began to doubt DI Burke. The investigation was moving too slow, and Clarence had told her that with missing children there was a very small window to work in. Every hour that passed increased her fear and trepidation.

'Who would have taken Emily?' Clarence asked when they were alone.

'I don't know,' she answered helplessly and ashamed.

'We have to think, Ava. It doesn't make sense.'

'Why? Do you think I have something to do with this?' Her eyes widened, and there was hysteria in her elevated voice.

'Of course not,' Clarence answered forcefully just before the phone rang. It was DI Burke; Ava's story had checked out. Clarence told Burke they hadn't received any calls regarding a ransom either, and there was no money to be had in the family that would warrant kidnapping of a child. Clarence wondered if DI Burke suspected Ava, whether she believed Ava had killed her daughter and was trying to cover it up, but truth be told he knew he couldn't ask. After hanging up the phone, he walked outside, and he paced up and down the road, Ava peering from her curtain. Clarence caught her trying to be discreet. DI Burke informed Clarence of her meeting with Dr. Ken Hopper and asked if Clarence knew anything about the depression from her separation. It was clear; the father had been the reason behind Ava's depression, and Clarence felt devastated he hadn't addressed the issue with Ava sooner. That was a guilt he would have to carry.

As he opened the front door, Ava stood there with sunken eyes staring back at him. Her makeup was gone, her hair was unwashed, and her clothes were dishevelled. She struggled to catch her breath as she numbed in agony.

'You're going to tell me everything about Emily's father, right here, right now.'

CHAPTER 9

Digging up the past

'Clarence, you don't understand!' Ava pleaded.

'You're right, that's why you're going to tell me everything, right now.' Clarence's eyes pierced Ava with a cold stare; she swallowed deeply and looked side to side as if she was about to make a confession.

'I can't,' she whimpered.

'GOD DAMNIT, AVA!' Clarence snarled, 'Emily is missing, and I think you're withholding information about her whereabouts. Her father is our only lead.'

'It's not her father,' she conceded.

'How can you be sure of that?' he begged.

'He went up north with his bit of stuff,' Ava shrugged, 'I don't want to discuss it.'

'It was obviously something worth discussing with Dr. Hopper though, wasn't it?'

'DI Burke….' Ava guessed, 'she had no right to sniff around.'

'DI Burke is investigating the disappearance of a missing child. She, as any other Detective, is following leads, and a prime suspect is standing right in front of me.'

'ME?' Ava gasped. 'Fine. His name is Daniel Grayson.'

Clarence grabbed the phone and dialled for DI Burke. As the phone rang, Clarence paced the living room twirling the cord between his fingers and murmured, 'pickup, pickup.' As DI Tenley Burke answered the phone, Clarence instructed, 'Burke, get an APW on a Daniel Grayson.' He then hung up without further adieu.

'Clarence, what's going on?'

'If he's still in the country, we've put an all-ports warning out on him. If you can give me any information on his appearance, the APW circulates a suspect's description to airports, ports, and international railway stations to detect an offender or suspect leaving the country.'

'Oh…all right….I have a photograph somewhere, hang on just a minute.' Ava rushed upstairs to rifle through her office drawers in search of a photograph; a photo she had taken two years ago of Emily and her father when they went to Brighton for Father's day.

'Dr. Hopper told DI Burke that Daniel wanted custody of Emily, is that true?' he asked.

'Well yes, as any parent would. That's why he left. He knew any judge would always side with the mother, and he couldn't afford the legal battle. It's as I told you, he left with some floozy.'

Ava, overwhelmed and in tears, stared at her reflection in her bathroom mirror and realised she was a shadow of her former self.

DI Burke and Clarence kept in constant contact. After Clarence's brief shower, he and Burke met up an hour later after Clarence issued the APW on Daniel. DI Burke had some information.

On his way to the meeting, Clarence wandered between the expressionless souls that sauntered through the town, each side of the street is adorned with a variety of shops from antiques to jewellery stores, fashion boutiques and kiosks with London souvenirs for the tourists. A multitude of accents would enthusiastically flock towards the stores as Clarence hustled past them. Quiet alleyways, built many years ago stretched high into the darkening sky, and as the lampposts began to flicker, he was almost at his destination. The buildings loomed over him as he quickened his pace along the cobblestone road, and the neighbouring sounds ricocheted off the buildings. After a quick glance over his shoulders and again in front of him, he left the deserted street and felt his heart slow in pace.

The derelict shop blended with the theme of the town, a place you wouldn't want to stay in for any length of time. But, inside the creaking floorboards and vine covered walls, there were more meetings and sales than any shop. DI Burke had known about this little black market, and it provided the perfect cover for an ad hoc rendezvous.

'What is this place?' Clarence asked whilst scouting his eyes in every corner.

'Shush, come here and take off your hat. You look like a cop.' Burke grabbed Clarence's arm and pulled him into a secluded part of the abandoned building. 'It was the only place I felt sure there would be no prying eyes or anyone listening,' she whispered.

'But there are people here.'

'People here don't care about cops and robbers. Sure, there is some illegal trading going on, but for the most part, people here just want to make sure their kids are fed. Look around, Clarence; they're trading food that would otherwise be tossed into the bins. It's the roughest of the rough. We'll be able to talk. Pull up a chair; I've got something you might find interesting.'

'It's dirty.'

'Sit on this,' she answered whilst handing him her scarf. 'You might find this interesting.'

'About Daniel Grayson?'

'Yes. Daniel Grayson, forty-six years of age and CEO of Grayson Construction.'

'He's a builder?' Clarence asked and nodded.

'Now, what I find most interesting is, imagine this. You're this CEO with a highly tense position running one of the country's largest construction companies, but you bury that tension so you can get up and do the same thing over and over again, day after day.'

'I'm not following you on this one, Burke.'

'He must have brought some of that tension home; it would be impossible not to. Perhaps he is a tense parent, a controlling husband, eventually imploding that home life he worked so eagerly for. It would lead to bitterness and a lot of resentment.' Burke was the perfect flip side of a coin for Landon, who himself tried to be a guileless and open character who tended to look at people with rose-tinted spectacles. Landon came across as an honourable man who often said to Burke that she had a nature so honest and transparent that to conceal her emotions would be impossible.

On the whole, it would be Burke that was a simple woman, but not a stupid one. She understood Landon, sometimes more than he understood himself, and, more often than not, she could draw the wrong conclusion, hence why he kept some details to himself.

'But, my genius, you don't know that's how it went down with him and Ava, do you, Burke?' he exclaimed.

'No, that is still an enigma. But, has Ava ever told you anything about him? I did a background check and he looks clean, every transaction and whereabouts justified…that was until six months ago.'

'Six months ago?'

'Yes…I know…when Ava's depression started.'

'I always did say you had a genius for stating the clear obvious,' he chuckled.

'Clarence, I'm not finished yet.'

'An obvious fact I clearly neglected. Do continue, please pardon my interruption.'

'We don't know yet what the pivotal moment was six months ago. However, Barclays recorded a credit card transaction in Harlow.'

As her last words left her mouth the wind snapped a window pane closed, making Clarence jump in his seat. The fancy architecture of the derelict building gave it that old fashioned horror movie-esque appearance, and nothing good ever comes from buildings that had endured seasons of beatings. It had been empty for generations, and no one knew who owned it or why it hadn't been demolished or refurbished. It was a gaunt shell of a building with mostly broken glass, but Clarence could imagine it once being some grand mansion with fancy mullioned windows and thick oak doors. It was such a shame some yobs had moved in and allowed the damp to move in too. The heavily patterned wallpaper hung loose from the walls, but at least there weren't used syringes and other drug paraphernalia.

To the locals, buildings like this were so alluring, and they could carry out their dealings uninterrupted as no one in their right mind would actually want to be anywhere near it.

'Harlow. Where have I heard that place mentioned before?' Clarence wondered whilst stroking his chin.

'It's where the Hendersons used to live.'

CHAPTER 10

"The four most dangerous words in investing are:
"This time it's different"

DI Burke and DCI Landon remained at the abandoned building for another hour. Apparently Landon's neighbour, Wallace Henderson, was already under the watchful eye of Scotland Yard, and Wallace had been gathering evidence on his previous colleagues in exchange for leniency.

According to Scotland Yard's file on Wallace, back in the 1950s, Wallace Henderson had procured a job as a stockbroker for London's Richmond Stockbrokers, employed under a man named Andrew Page, who had enticed him with a sex-fuelled go-lucky stockbroker culture, and who had trained him into believing the one and only true goal of being a stockbroker is to make money for himself. Thanks to Wallace's charming yet aggressive approach, his commissions were rolling in, and he made himself a considerable fortune; coincidently that's when he met his wife, Claudia. The two embarked on their own adventure, founding Arden Brokers. Claudia's get-rich-quick scheme and Wallace's hard sell catapulted their small company into success where he inflated the prices of stocks from somewhat bankrupt companies by misleading clients with positive statements in order to sell at the augmented price. *Cheeky bastard.*

The two slid into a decadent lifestyle of drugs and prostitutes developing an elite social circle, and that's when Scotland Yard had them on their radar and began investigating Arden Brokers. Wallace illegally made £2 million in one hour upon securing the stock market launch of McCarthy Limited which brought Wallace and his company under further scrutiny from Scotland Yard. In order to hide his fortune, Wallace opened up an off-shore account in the Cayman Islands, a British territory, where the account process is usually fairly simple. In most cases, accounts can be set up without ever travelling to the islands. It's one of the choice favourites among people that have £200,000 or more they intend to hide, the Cayman Islands having a reputation as a stable and safe place to store assets. There, there are tax loopholes, and the wealthy and nefarious take their money there to protect it from laws and taxes they don't want to adhere to.

But, when one of Arden Brokers' employees was apprehended by the police on an unrelated charge, Claudia advised her husband to lay low. Unfortunately, the employee had already squealed and informed Scotland Yard. Wallace was served a three year sentence in a minimum security prison, and Claudia threatened divorce. But after just twenty-four months he was out, sobered up, and decided to start fresh.

'Unfortunately, he was at the top of his game. He ran a central greed equals power monetary scheme which had a wide base of victims below. His notion, as relayed to his clients, that "We all win", was a load of tosh. For every one person high up, there were many trodden on, living hand-to-mouth as the waged slaves of the financial system, and one of these that believed in Wallace and his gift of the gab was financial tycoon Daniel Grayson and his company, Grayson Construction.'

'Jesus…' Clarence Landon rubbed his hand across his mouth and rubbed his forehead as he placed his head into his hands.

'There's more,' the DI stated.

She continued to explain Wallace's involvement with the social elite, and his contacts in the financial industry procured women who were often sexually abused.

'And has Wallace been charged with procuring prostitutes?' Clarence dreaded to ask.

'Not as of yet, but the Met strongly believe he's a go-between for an international paedophile ring.'

'That bastard! Burke, I'm going to strangle that fucker.'

'No, you won't. We can't touch him. I'm under strict instructions on this one, Clarence; I could lose my job if they knew I had even told you. I just thought you should know.'

Mr Henderson had given evidence that he "lent" girls to people in power in order to ingratiate himself into their social circles.

'We're monitoring his movements, Clarence, but he hasn't made a move in the last six months.'

'Does he know we have eyes on him?'

'Yes, he does.'

CHAPTER 11

Never talk to strangers

The disappearance of Emily Willows had attracted widespread media and police attention throughout the United Kingdom. It quickly attracted numerous suspects, but it also came with theories and hoaxes. New leads and clues were reported almost daily, and there were regular headlines in both print and broadcast media in hopes someone remembered seeing something, somewhere. It would be credited to changing Britain's lifestyle for years to come, forcing parents to believe their children could no longer play in the parks, go the beaches or simply be safe when unsupervised in public.

The police had quickly and efficiently organised searches in and around the Willows' residence, based on the assumption that Emily had simply gone out in the evening looking for her mother. The search expanded to neighbouring buildings and villages, then railways and bus stations, to now the assumption of a kidnapping. Within forty-eight hours the entire nation had become aware of Emily's disappearance. Within four days the Daily Post had the headline:

Willows child now feared as victim of sex crime.

This highlighted the situation and created frenzy among the public that she had been kidnapped and possibly murdered by a sex-offender. It was established on the day of the disappearance that Emily was carrying only one item, a teddy bear, and to this date, neither Emily nor the teddy bear had been found.

DI Burke had found several witnesses who had seen the mild-mannered, four foot three inch youngster on Tresham's lane, which was two streets behind the Willows' house, in the company of a tall, thin- haired man in his mid-50s. She was described as being relaxed as she walked with him sometime later. The police estimated the time to be around 21:00.

Ava Willows described her child as shy, and to be confident around a complete stranger seemed out of character. DCI Landon theorised that perhaps the stranger had previously been known to Emily, maybe she and Ava had met him on a previous visit somewhere, and the girl had grown to trust him. A remark in the household which had been deemed insignificant at the time supported the theory. Emily had told her mother that she had a boy-friend. Ava assumed that she meant a play friend at school and took no further notice until the disappearance and the questioning by DI Burke.

A shopkeeper at Cake 'n' Bake Bakery had reported that Emily had bought some carrot cake. She remembered suggesting it to the undecided youngster who remarked she didn't like vegetables. The lady told how she persuaded the young girl by explaining to her that carrots were used as a sweetener for desserts. She further helped convince her by telling her the history of the use of the vegetable. Since the 10th century, Arabian cooks would use the carrot to turn their desserts to life; being unable to afford the more expensive honey. During World War II, the necessity of food rationing forced the cake eating British nation to get creative with what was available at the time, and low and behold the carrot cake was lifted. Of course the girl laughed, but the shopkeeper felt it was the offer of the cream cheese frosting, an American twist, that persuaded the child in the end.

'Quite the conversation you had,' DI Burke inquired.

'Yes, she was in the shop for quite some minutes and was *very* undecided. I just wanted to help,' the shopkeeper answered.

'So if Emily wasn't familiar with buying cakes and pastries, how did she pay?'

'I don't think she had ever set foot in a bakery before. She paid with a one pound note,' the shopkeeper shrugged.

DI Burke and DCI Landon viewed this as further evidence that Emily had been in the company of somebody else, and they had in fact given her the money. Two reasons; the shop keeper had never seen the child before, so why would Emily visit this particular shop, and secondly, her mother never left any money in the house. Ava had her purse with her at the time of the disappearance, and gave Emily only a few shillings on a school day; enough for lunch. DI Burke believed the pound had been given to Emily by somebody else.

Landon and Burke kept their theories to themselves. It had been only a decade since the discovery of motivations behind abductions had shifted from ransom money to satisfying sexual desires. Of course, paedophilia has always existed, but it wasn't until the 1960s that society, previously too prim and proper, were ready to acknowledge or even publicise the very thought.

CHAPTER 12

"If you want to keep a secret, you must also hide it
from yourself",
George Orwell

"Old Harlow" was a village founded in the early medieval period consisting of Victorian buildings, and after World War II, a new town called Harlow was built to ease the overcrowding in London that had occurred due to the devastation the bombing had caused during The Blitz. Along with other towns, Harlow was part of the New Towns Act in 1946 with a plan drawn up by Sir Frederick Gibberd, an English architect, town planner and landscape designer who wanted to respect the existing landscape but create a couple of wedges, later known as Green Wedges, to cut through the town and separate neighbours. Gibberd worked alongside many of the country's leading post-war architects to design the town's buildings. One of his own being Trompe-l'oeil Terrace in Orchard Croft; a pair of curved terraces which won a British Housing Award in 1951 and one of the country's first modern style residential tower blocks – The Lawn was also constructed in 1951.

With Harlow having a population of roughly 90,000 inhabitants, DCI Landon wondered if he would find any information about a single man. Harlow had been built out of the idealism of the post-war Labour Government, being one of eight new towns solely designed to provide fairly decent housing to survivors of London's Blitz. The 50s and 60s were pioneering eras and Harlow landed itself chalking up a series of firsts. Mag Barret was a journalist who had recently moved to the town and covered many local newspapers including the Harlow Citizen, Harlow Star, and the Harlow News. As Landon picked up a local newspaper, he flicked through the pages whilst he sipped on a coffee in the high-street, and he wondered why he hadn't visited before. Harlow was the new place to go for the young, ambitious, and family starters, and it soon earned the name "pram town" as Harlow gave the feeling that things could be done in Harlow that couldn't be done elsewhere. To others, speaking to the locals, it came across that Harlow was their little prairie.

Sir Frederick Gibberd was obsessed with the idea that a town should have its own individual personality, and he thought he could do it only by grasping an idea of the landscape and basing the construction on that; the form of the town dictating its structure more than anything, thus offering it as a form of art once completed. Richard Costain, the Chairman of Harlow Development Agency, stated that apart from their own architectural staff, they have about forty different firms of architects; they would give them an area of about four to six hundred houses and allow them considerable freedom to use their imagination and their own ideas within each area. One of the firms was Grayson Construction.

Landon drove past Harlow's new sign; Harlow New Town with the coat of arms emblazoned on the right of the sign. He smiled as he admired the quaint town. Locals speculated that Grayson Construction was at the Old Harlow fire station; a station that had survived two world wars. A horse and cart originally had been the mode of transport for the crew with the horses being housed at the George hotel. Rumour had it that this tiny single bay station was little more than a shed, and it had a smaller fire engine called a Bedford fire truck that was purposely built for smaller buildings. Landon was excited at the idea. He questioned whether finding Grayson or seeing a real life fire engine was going to be the pivotal moment of this journey, and as he pulled up to 82 High Street, Landon saw the words Grayson Construction painted on the side of a cream Ford Transit.

'Can I help you?' questioned one of the workers.

'Perhaps,' answered Landon. The worker seemed obviously irritated watching Landon step out of his Bristol. He observed Landon, who took utmost pride in his appearance, walk towards him carrying himself with great dignity, and knew that even a speck of dust may cause him more discomfort than a bullet. As Landon flashed his badge, the worker glanced over his shoulder.

'I don't know nufin',' he said.

'I should, perhaps, Sir, tell you a little more about myself. I am Detective Chief Inspector Landon.'

'Is that meant to mean somefin'?' The worker remained unmoved.

'I'm looking for a Daniel Grayson. I believe he's your boss?' Landon closed his eyes determinedly. He admitted to the worker that Grayson is wanted by the police in regard to a kidnapping investigation, at which the worker was left speechless. Landon believed he could trust the worker's account for Grayson in that he hadn't seen nor heard from him in the last six months, and in actual fact the company was relying on small building jobs just so they could feed their families. Landon devised two possible answers; Grayson really has moved up north with "some floozy" and left everything behind, or he is laying low, perhaps with his daughter in tow - the latter being more probable.

'Any chance I can take a gander at that old Bedford fire truck?' Landon pointed out.

'Cor, blimey, I didn't think a man of your sorts in that posh car would be interested in an old fire engine,' the worker answered in relief, 'Ya know come to think of it….'

'A commendable exercise...' Landon smiled as he interrupted.

'What?' The worker asked, obviously annoyed.

'Thinking, do continue….you were saying?' Landon glanced his eye over the red fire engine, 'My, what a wonderful piece of machinery,' Landon stated in awe.

'Yeah, that's what old man Grayson used to say. Apparently, it brought back memories of a place he used to frequent when he was a boy.'

'You're from London, aren't you?' Landon asked the worker.

'Yes.'

'Did you know, there were no fire brigades before The Great Fire of London?'

The worker looked at Landon with a perplexed expression, but regardless, Landon continued. 'That was the 1666 London blaze that burned for days on a long dry summer. It tore through packed homes, and the flammable building materials were just a recipe for disaster. Amazing what a stray bakery spark can cause, tragic.'

'Yeah 'course, was just testin' you there.' The worker stroked the fire engine as they walked around it.

'Where did your boss frequent that had fire

engines?

'South East somewhere, Surrey maybe?'

'It is not the man who has too little, but the man who craves more, that is poor. Do forgive me; I need to make a phone call,' Landon mumbled.

Landon accessed the nearest phone box and DI Burke answered on the third ring.

'Landon, how's Harlow?' She laughed.

'Interesting, I can see why Grayson Construction is up here with all the new development.'

'Did you find him?' Burke gasped.

'No, and no one has seen him for the last six months either.'

'What if he's dead, Landon?' Burke queried.

'Your imagination has too much rein, Burke,' he answered.

'Honestly,   for   Grayson's   disappearance,   the simplest explanation is always the most likely.'

'That is usually my line. I must be rubbing off on you. "If fact will not fit the theory – let the theory go".' mumbled Landon.

'Pardon me?' she questioned.

'You have arrived at a conclusion much faster than I would have permitted myself to do, but not one dismissible,' Landon pointed out. 'I'll be back in a few hours,' he stated before hanging up.

Landon's next port of call took him to the new police station that opened in 1957 in Crown Gate. As he walked through the front door, a detective caught his eye. Landon would hardly admit that one of his first ports of calls upon reaching Harlow had been to look up his old friend, Anthony Jeeves. Jeeves laughed wholeheartedly when he saw Landon walk through the door.

Jeeves was a fifty something year old copper with

a spade shaped beard, crow's feet, and blood freckled jade eyes from his whiskey days, but his hoarse voice hadn't changed.

'Ay up, Duck' he applauded. 'Landon, my dear friend.' Jeeves stood. He was looking wonderfully well and not much had aged him in the ten years that had passed since Landon last saw him. Landon beamed at Jeeves.

'How nice to see you! Are you here on a job?'

Landon smiled and squinted his eyes.

'No, no, I assure you I am here purely in my private capacity. How are you my friend?' Landon asked.

'Great, you're looking well, Landon. You've hardly aged at all. In fact, I would almost say that you have fewer grey hairs than when I saw you last,' Jeeves eyed Landon up and down as he patted him on the side of the arm.

Landon smiled. 'That is quite possible, Jeeves.'

'How is that so? You're not Benjamin Button in disguise are you?'

'Not quite,' Landon laughed.

'But surely, what you are saying is scientifically impossible?'

'Not in the slightest,' Landon grinned.

'Extraordinary. Do tell, old chap. We could all do with some youthful lifting around here. What's your potion?' Jeeves laughed.

'As I remembered, Jeeves, the years have not changed you. Your perception is impeccable.'

Landon leaned in close to Jeeves' ear and whispered, 'Hilltone Hair dye with a touch of Duke.'

'Landon!' he cried. 'You dye your hair?'

'Ah the realisation hits you, well done. Now don't tell everyone.' Landon nodded his head as Jeeves recovered. 'Tell me, Jeeves, do you still have connections?'

'I see it is not just your fashion that is fastidious. I'll admit my friend, I am coming up to retirement, but for you, anything. Tell me, what do you need?' Jeeves' frown of perplexity deepened across his forehead. Landon took Jeeves aside and suddenly he gave a decisive nod. He handed Landon a folder, which Landon took with interest.

Anthony Jeeves hadn't remained in contact as much as he wished with Clarence since the inception of his force in 1947, with Clarence just starting his police career. Jeeves, having moved from his hometown in Staffordshire, served in the RAF during the Second World War and returned to police duties at the cessation of hostilities. By the 1950s, the rise in criminality increased in the post-war period, and the number of recorded crimes rose tenfold since the '20s. Jeeves was a DS at the time that two burglars attempted a break-in at a confectionery manufacturer. Jeeves gained entry but was quickly seized by one of the burglars and was shot in the shoulder by the other. Upon armed uniformed officers arriving, Clarence included, a Constable by the name of Jones was shot dead. DS Jeeves was awarded the George Cross for his role in the incident, and Landon received the British Empire Medal.

'Thank you, Jeeves, I owe you one.'

'If I remember correctly, I was indebted to you. I'm still with the old girl and will let her know you dropped by, and Landon…don't leave it another ten years, will ya' old chap! Keep rocking those sideburns.' Jeeves winked.

Landon left before Jeeves reverted back to his Second World War days how he described an altercation with the opposition, "I grabbed him by the neck and I said I'd fucking have him. There was claret everywhere, I tell ya". How much of that was true Clarence didn't know, but Jeeves could get pretty brutal when he re-enacted the moment.

Landon made tracks towards the Henderson's old home. The folder contained information about Wallace, Claudia, and Arden Brokers. He had to see the property for himself to gain a sense of reality. He wondered what his faithful sidekick Burke would say. Clarence valued her imaginative approach to cases and often gave rise to creative hypotheses that Clarence would often mock. *Oh how my dear friend would have enjoyed this trip, what extravagant incompetence she would utter.* As far as Landon was concerned, Burke was not necessarily a great detective, but she served him well over the last ten years. She was absolutely scrupulous, and although she lacked Landon's intellect, or so he thought, he'd often compliment her on her ability to remember facts and details about cases, even if her account of how they were solved deplored Landon the majority of the time. Only now had he realised how much he missed their working relationship.

Clarence and Burke hadn't seen each other for about the last two years. Their seemingly controversial working relationship was deemed as a conflict of interest. But what their superintendent at the time hadn't realised was, Burke never really allowed herself to get too close to anyone. She avoided emotional attachment, perhaps being so afraid of dying and death it seemed like a bad move, and that anything she formed would never last. Burke started her police career after her father was involved in a series of murders in which victims had been brutally butchered. She was attacked by the murderer in their own home. Her father had learned of his family's imminent danger and burst into the house moments before the assailant could carry out his task. Together, Burke and her father managed to handcuff the killer, who was ultimately sentenced to death for multiple murders and assaults.

CHAPTER 13

The truth doesn't cost anything, but a lie could
cost you everything

Clarence Landon had enjoyed being on the road with his Bristol, painted in British racing green. During 1953, the car manufacturer Bristol unveiled its model 405 to the world, and for Landon it was something rather special; a four door coupé with an unmatched style of the time. With a top speed of 110mph and 0-60 in twelve seconds, the 405 was miles ahead of any other four door vehicle of the era, and it proved to be a subject of mockery among Clarence's colleagues. For Tenley Burke, she admired Clarence; his peculiar mincing walk and the many nuances of his character. Although she viewed Clarence as a very anally-retentive, fastidious person that was extremely irritating, he had an unusual appeal, a charming aspect, and sometimes could be humorous.

Landon pulled up outside the station to inform Burke of his return from Harlow. His smile stretched from ear to ear as he came to a grinding halt. He leaned to roll down the window as he saw Burke.

'Tenley, get in,' he shouted.

'Clarence, enjoy the trip?'

'As a matter of fact, yes. I also happened to pop in and see Anthony Jeeves. You remember him, right?'

'Jeeves? I bet you were welcomed as much as a fart in a space suit?' Tenley laughed.

'Interesting… If you forgive me for being personal, Detective Inspector Burke, but there is a missing child, my child might I add. And I, Detective

Chief Inspector Landon, am not amused.'

'I was only taking the Mickey Bliss, Landon. It's been a long day, I've been up since seven, I haven't eaten since then, and all that was left at the station was a stale cream cheese bagel. It wasn't even proper cheese!' she gasped.

'What's a bagel? Never mind! No more is to be said on the matter. Tomorrow is a new day, and I've got a new lead. I'll pick you up at 08:00am sharp.' Landon stated.

'Yes Sir.' Tenley nodded in compliance.

As Clarence pulled up outside the Willows' residence, he glanced towards the Henderson's and grunted as he saw Claudia peering out from behind the curtain. Ava was standing behind the front door with a glimmer of hope shimmering from her eyes as he entered.

'Clarence, I was afraid you wouldn't return!' she said as she fidgeted whilst rubbing her hands together.

'I was called away on a case,' he answered.

It was a few minutes after nine when Landon reached Ava's home, and he had purposely delayed entering the house. As Ava interrogated his whereabouts, he hung up his hat and trench coat that had taken solely as a precaution to colder weather when he travelled north to Harlow. If he told the truth, he was upset and concerned, and he never was too good at pretending as he foresaw the events that would unfold in the coming weeks.

'What case? I've still not heard anything about Emily. Have you given up? Moved on?' Ava's anger accelerated. 'Where have you been?'

'I've been to Harlow.'

'What's in Harlow?' Ava recoiled.

'I've been tracking Daniel Grayson,' Clarence walked towards the kitchen to heat up the kettle. Ava stood motionless and slowly followed behind.

'I told you Daniel was way up north.'

'I know what you said, Ava, but Daniel is nearby, I can sense it.'

'That's impossible.' Ava shook her head disbelieving the news. 'Did you see him?'

'No, but I will tomorrow. I will find him *and* Emily,' he answered confidently.

'You think Emily is with Daniel?' Ava asked in a panicked manner. Everything Ava would say from this moment onwards would be determined by whether she would look guilty in the disappearance of her daughter, or just a concerned mother.

'Yes,' he answered.

Clarence boiled the kettle for the second time. He was already filled to the brim with tea and busied himself cleaning the dishes in the kitchen before settling down for the evening. He glanced again at Ava whose eyes had illuminated, but her skin remained pale and matte. In all his years playing poker, he recognised a mask of defiance. He could see the slight pinkness of her cheeks, but she remained nonchalant. *What is she hiding?* He wondered.

A moment of silence moved through the house. Both Clarence and Ava moved back and forth passing one another. The faucet dripped into the sink, each drip reverberating around the kitchen like a cymbal that neither person attempted to stop. Conversation had come to a halt. What more was there to talk about?

Telling Ava anything about the case went against

the grain. His dread pushed him like a strong wind, his stomach churned knowing what the outcome might be. His teeth ground together, and his face went stern. As Clarence swirled the spoon around the rim of the mug, he swallowed hard but executed his words without agitation.

'Ava…,' he started just as the phone rang.

The phone reverberated on the dial and as Ava scooped it up, she spoke into it, listened for a moment, and then handed it to Landon.

'Landon? You there?' the voice sternly requested.

'Yes.'

'Superintendent Floyd, I suggest you get your arse down to the station asap.'

'Yes Sir.' Landon put the phone down, gulped the last of his tea, and headed for the door. He grabbed his coat and keys and slammed the door behind him without a word to Ava.

CHAPTER 14

It all depends on how we look at things

Clarence Landon sat outside the office door of Superintendent Floyd. He could hear chattering behind it, along with the tapping of the typewriter by the receptionist.

'Won't be long now,' she stated.

Part of the room was painted grey, other walls had oak panelling and dark anodised aluminium windows. Floyd's office gave that minimalist look that accentuated the pattern of the carpet and the sofa in which Landon sat. Floyd looked important and established, but Landon had met him only a handful of times. As the door opened, Landon stood to attention, and Detective Inspector Burke walked out.

'Landon, come in,' Floyd gestured with his hand for Landon to take a seat. 'How are you holding up, Landon?'

'All right, given the circumstances,' Clarence answered.

'Yes. That's why I have called you in here today. How's Ava?' Floyd leaned forward. He was stern and by-the-book. His previous encounters with Landon had been strained, and Landon felt he always had to justify why his actions had merit. This time it felt no different.

'She's distraught,' Clarence replied.

'I can imagine,' Floyd nodded sympathetically.

'With all due respect, Sir, I'm sure I'm not here for your condolences?' Landon questioned.

'That's right. It has been brought to my attention

that you have been growing increasingly impulsive, and despite your ad-hoc adventures...'

'If you're referring to Harlow?' Clarence interrupted.

'Yes, I'm referring to Harlow. What the hell were you thinking? In fact, don't answer that. As Detective Chief Inspector you have successfully held major investigations, and your work has been an asset. How long have you been with us now, Landon?'

'Quite a while.'

'This place is the benchmark for excellent police work across the country, and you have an impeccable record.'

'Thank you,' Landon nodded.

'And given this, as you're quite smart, despite your arrogance, I'd like to give you the opportunity to explain why you have gone above the head of your superior.' Floyd leaned back in his chair. He personified the black and white morality. He wasn't really interested in the why, and when it came to criminals, he either wanted them in jail or dead. Landon wondered if Floyd had a good reason to call him out or he just wanted to be mean; he couldn't decide.

'I'm not going by a police procedural rule book here,' Clarence started.

'No need to state the obvious, Landon.'

'I was investigating the whereabouts of Emily Willows' father.'

'And did you find him?' Floyd squinted his eyes. He had always been a straight arrow, and although he never really believed in the decisions Landon had made, he never actively hindered them. He just wanted to be a part of them.

'Not yet, but I've found links leading to the

involvement of child trafficking. I'll know more when I interview him.'

'Interview him? Look Landon, it isn't our job to commiserate with criminals, it is our job to prosecute and execute where necessary.'

'I understand.'

'Tell me, Landon, how did you get ever so close to the Krays?' Floyd queried.

'By being a sneaky bastard.'

'I like it! Good, now fuck off. Come back when you've more news. Oh, and Landon, you've got Burke to thank this time.' Floyd waved Clarence to leave the room.

'Thank you, Sir.' Landon rose from his chair and shook the superintendent's hand.

Floyd was referring to the early 60s where London had turned violent with police clashing with hostile protesters that were making newspaper headlines. The Metropolitan Police realised a separate elite unit was required for public disorder, and by 1965 they had formed the Special Patrol Group. Of course, Clarence's punch first and ask questions later approach proved him an ideal candidate, and here he received specialised training that ordinary officers on the beat didn't get. His duties included gathering intelligence on known robbers, and one of his notable investigations included his squad's role in the gathering of evidence against the Kray twins.

DI Burke at the time was working with the Kidnap Unit of the Serious and Organised Crime Command when she and Landon crossed paths.

Clarence wasn't quite sure why he had to thank Burke, but she was next on his list of people to see.

Burke was waiting downstairs in the cafeteria and gestured with her head Landon was to join her.

'How did it go?' Burke asked.

'What was all that about?'

'No idea! My guess, Jeeves whistled on you.' Burke shrugged.

'What did you tell Floyd?' Landon queried.

'I told him the truth, that we're looking for Emily.'

'And...' he urged.

'And you had some theories you wanted to look into.'

'I thought as much,' Landon nodded.

'Look, Landon, between you and me, your attitude is going to eventually bite you in the arse.'

'I want to interview Wallace,' Landon declared.

Burke was far less detached than Landon, and she was pretty good at staying professional during interviews. She knew that interviewing Wallace would strike a very touchy subject if Landon was to bring up children, but she did agree with him.

'We should be using every resource we have and talking to the smartest people in the field,' Burke nodded.

'Floyd can't like everything we do. If we're going to find out the whys, we have to push some buttons and go straight to the source.' Clarence stated.

'Do you think Wallace will crack?' Burke asked.

'I hope so, but psychopaths are convinced that there is nothing wrong with them, so they're virtually impossible to study,' Landon smiled at the thought.

'You think he's a psychopath?' Burke's forehead wrinkled as her eyes widened at Clarence's statement.

'Don't you? How do you define psychopathy?'

'I've never really given it any thought, Clarence. Why would you want to study one - that is if Wallace is a sicko.'

'Wouldn't you want to know what motivates a

killer, a child kidnapper, a rapist, and so forth?'

'No, not really.' Burke shrugged her shoulders whilst she cupped her black coffee. She never really gave any thought to why criminals do what they do or how they think, and she humoured Clarence for his profiling insights as a means to help solve crimes and prevent further attacks.

'These people are just mad, Clarence. It's as simple as that.'

'I don't believe it is. How can we understand mad if we don't know how mad thinks? Imagine what it takes for someone to bludgeon someone, or that desire to control, or the emotion of arousal at that moment they take a life. The cognitive process to butcher or shame someone's body, how could you possibly get that from words printed in a report?'

Detective Chief Inspector Landon was Burke's superior, but she felt comfortable enough with their working relationship to pick him up where she felt necessary, but Landon had a point.

'Let's bring him in then. Drink up, Clarence you've got results to deliver. Floyd demands it.'

CHAPTER 15

Inside the criminal mind

Wallace Henderson sat alone inside the dark, empty room. It was the last room at the end of the corridor, and as Clarence and Burke walked towards it, the fluorescent lights flickered on and off. Wallace shuffled his feet back and forth whilst his skeletal fingers tapped the top of the table. Landon and Burke observed him for a few moments through the one-way window whilst Landon steadied his breathing and contemplated how the next few minutes would pan out.

The interview room was tasteful in a nondescript way. There was nothing to cause offence no matter what the interviewee's personal tastes might be; four bland, washed out, grey concrete walls, and a bare bulb hanging in the centre of the ceiling, and a plastic chair and table that looked about as comfortable as a park bench.

Wallace Henderson sat alone, his eyes wandering from one wall to another, his stature making the table and chair look like something that had been given to the station from pre-school liquidation.

Wallace remained seated whilst Landon walked into the room carrying a dossier and tape recorder. He skipped the introductory normalities and got straight to the point, pressing record.

'This is Detective Chief Inspector Clarence Landon interviewing Wallace Henderson. Can you please state your name for the record?'

'I am Wallace Henderson.'

'Thank you. Now I'd like to ask you a few questions if that would be all right with yourself?'

'Clarence, you look tired. I'm sure you don't want to be here anymore than I do. Mind letting me know what's going on here?' Wallace asked as he lifted his hands. 'Am I under arrest?'

'You're not under arrest, Wallace. I just need to clarify a few things if that is all right. We know your involvement with Daniel Grayson, the father of the missing child, Emily Willows, and I also know about your three year stint in prison. So, shall we start again?'

'Then you'll also be aware I'm a free man,' Wallace answered smugly.

'We're hoping you can shed some light on the matter and perhaps, in exchange for your cooperation, we can come to some agreement?'

Wallace laughed. 'Police find me intriguing because they can talk to me. Some find they can engage in more conversation with me than their own families.'

'Is that a fact?'

'Sure. I watch all the police dramas on TV. I know what you're doing,' Wallace folded his arms tightly against his chest.

'Ever watched The Avengers?' Landon smiled.

'Are you kidding me? Huge fan! Got a great amount of insight right there,' Wallace laughed.

'Really?' Clarence jotted down notes on his notepad.

'Come to think of it, you and that sassy DI Burke are a bit like Cathy Gale and John Steed.'

'How is that?' Landon questioned.

'Well, the relationship between Steed and Gale was marked instantly by a sexual tension, and they, too, have a rocky working relationship. Gale is neither always appreciative of Steed's methods nor his habits, yet still the two have become quite close. And regardless of their policy of avoiding direct references of a possible romance between our two leads, I also picked up on the gimmicks, the mechanics of their procedures and the logic behind it. I'd always laugh and say to myself, I'd never allow myself to fall into that kind of trap.'

'What kind of trap are you referring to?'

'Openly discussing crimes. That's a classic,' Wallace nodded.

'Have you discussed your inclinations with anyone?' Clarence asked, but Wallace took no notice.

'What are you writing there, Clarence?' Wallace leaned forward.

'Just some notes.'

'Really…you know there are more people out there like me.'

'Like you? Do you classify yourself as a specific type of person?' Landon was onto something. Wallace Henderson was a classic narcissist. He enjoyed the attention, the notoriety. When Landon read his file, he realised all Wallace had wanted was to be recognised as someone of importance like his connections with the social elite.

'Oh yes, I mean don't quote me on this, but I'd like to say there could be in excess of fifty-five in this area for sure.'

'Fifty-five?'

'I'm not the embodiment of authority; I'm just someone who has been in the game for the last twenty-five years. Sure I have done time, but like I said, you've got to keep your friends close…Clarence, you couldn't throw me a cigarette, could you?' Wallace winked.

'Sure.' Clarence never smoked, but he knew Wallace liked to dabble. 'I read that you were a bit of a tycoon back in the '50s?' Clarence pressured.

Wallace laughed as he puffed on his cigarette.

'You could say that,' Wallace nodded.

'Is that when you met your wife, Claudia?'

'Yes, you could say part of the cover; you see no one questions a happily married couple. Be a bit odd if I was rich, handsome, and single, wouldn't it?' Wallace reminisced in the memory.

'Bit of an oxymoron that.' Clarence implied.

'How so?'

'Happily married, almost like saying happily dead.' Clarence smiled.

'Ah, yes, I see where you're coming from...'

'This cover, that's when you met Daniel Grayson from Grayson Construction?'

'It was.' Wallace's laughter came to a stop. He pierced Clarence with a stare.

'How long have you known Daniel Grayson?'

'At least ten years,' Wallace answered.

'A long time then? How did he respond to losing all his money?'

'Clarence, I'm happy to cooperate, but I really don't see how I can help.' Wallace stated as he stood.

'Unless you want to be arrested for procuring prostitutes, you'll sit your arse down.'

'I'm not in that game anymore.' Wallace sat down slowly.

'Was Daniel Grayson aware of your involvement in procuring women for your elite contacts? Did he ever procure women himself?'

'Good God no. Daniel was a pussy.'

'Was or is?'

'Why do you want to know so much about Daniel? Not the jealous-kind are you?'

'You got me, Wallace.' Clarence raised his hands. 'Another cigarette?' Clarence asked.

'Sure. Thank you.' Wallace smiled and nodded.

'You know, Wallace, I really feel we started off on the wrong foot. I mean, you move in next door, I didn't attend your dinner party, and all of a sudden we're mixed up in this scenario, and I find it difficult to square you with what you have been accused of.'

'Sure…' Wallace took it all in. He took the opportunity to corner DCI Landon and unmask him, understanding how gullible the DCI was, and that he was genuinely motivated. Landon had never spoken to a criminal before, and Wallace was a walking mystery that invited interpretation. Clarence had to read between the lines if he was to learn anything about Emily's whereabouts, because Wallace wasn't about to lay it out on a plate. Clarence allowed moments of pause, and he studied Wallace as he paced up and down the room. He watched his non-verbal behaviour, the way he moved compared to what he said with words. Depending on the subject, it caused a change in posture, but Landon noticed it was mainly in the eyes.

'Wallace, I have to ask, why the prostitutes? I mean, you have a beautiful wife.'

'Claudia is a great wife, but she's just that…a great wife. I'm not much to look at myself, but I have always gone after the pretty ones, you know, and after a while they lose their prettiness. You get what I'm saying? I bet you're no different, Clarence?'

'Oh yes, definitely,' Landon could cringe, but he remained professional and dug his fingernails into the palms of his hands hidden beneath the table before his next comment, 'I've always preferred them younger if I'm honest,' Clarence sniggered, but inside he felt sick.

Clarence's hand began to twitch, and Burke could see he was about to rise from his chair and give the accused a good hammering, so she entered the room. He felt her hand restraining his arm as she had seen the telltale sign and astutely foresaw what might come.

Burke admired Landon; she recognised the reputation the pair had acquired, and while she revelled in being the go-to shit kickers, it was wholly down to him.

'Easy, Landon,' she whispered. 'There's more than one way to shake a carbuncle.'

It certainly did the trick; Landon looked across at his female colleague with, once again, a look of perplexity, nodded, and she walked away.

'Clarence, you surprise me. Tell me, how young?' Wallace was intrigued.

'That would be telling... Tell me a little more about *your* fantasies.'

'Well, I like a bit of hair on the playing field, if you catch my drift and...'

'Wallace, I'm sorry to cut this interview short. I had no idea of the time. Interview suspended at sixteen hundred hours.' Clarence stopped recording and stood up.

'What did I say? Come on, Clarence, I thought we were buddies.'

'Another time maybe.' Landon opened the interview room door and looked at Burke. Her face was pale.

'Clarence...'

'Don't. Don't say a word.'

CHAPTER 16

"If you look down at me you will see a fool; if you look up at me you will see a God; if you look straight ahead at me you will see yourself."
Charles Manson

Clarence sat alone at the coffee shop, the fragrant aroma of perfume permeating the air among the ambiance of friendly chit-chat. Clarence could have his own seat, his own table, and have the sense of being social because there were so many tables and so little room. Yet, he had the confidence he could go over his contemplations alone and at his own leisure. Despite the coffee shop evoking a warm welcome, like that of your favourite grandma, Clarence was troubled by the interview with Wallace. He mulled over Wallace's answers and reactions; when he, Wallace, felt he was not in control of the situation, he folded his arms and became condescending. As Clarence viewed his notes that he laboriously jotted down, he realised it broke the natural flow of the discussion, Wallace lost his train of thought, and Clarence missed important answers to his questions. Clarence acknowledged that visibly taking notes in front of the interviewee was the first mistake.

Clarence always had a strong desire to understand criminals. What were their motivations, and was there a sexual component involved? Why did a perpetrator select that particular victim; was it an ad-hoc decision or was it planned? Clarence had always wondered and tried to ascertain the everyday aspects of a perpetrator's life – where they live, who did they know, where and if they worked, as well as what went on in the dark recesses of their minds. To most police officers, it was of little interest what kind of relationship a murderer might have with his mother, but Clarence always wondered if killers were born or created? Wallace hadn't been arrested. After all, he hadn't actually committed a crime, and the look on Burke's face when Clarence left the interview room certainly questioned the ethics of his methods. Wallace wasn't just going to clearly tell them if or why he was involved in Emily's disappearance, and Clarence started doubting whether his methods were going to achieve any significant results. After all, he has no discernible credentials. Clarence shook his head side to side and determinedly closed his eyes when he recalled the moment he faked empathy as a ploy for Wallace to open up. He could imagine Burke lecturing him and quoting Nietzsche, "He who fights with monsters should be careful lest he thereby become a monster. And if thou gaze long into an abyss, the abyss will also gaze into thee".

Burke arrived a few moments later and together they headed towards the Willows residence.

'Come on, Landon, this isn't like you.' Burke exclaimed as they drove.

'I have given my mind every chance, it has been cosseted, and I've slept a good solid seven hours to allow it to do its work. I even ate eggs for breakfast.' Landon shook his head.

'You'll work it out, Landon, your mind has never let you down,' Burke rubbed the side of Clarence's arm as she dropped him home; an empty home.

Ava laid there in her own filth. Clarence couldn't remember the last time she brushed her teeth or bathed. It was as if Ava had retreated inside herself, but her eyes were wide as if someone was about to give her the fatal blow to end her despair. Clarence could see she was trapped in her own psychosis, a psychosis pills couldn't change. She lived any mother's worst nightmare, and there was nothing he could do. He didn't know what to say, what to do, how he could make the situation any better.

'Ava….I…'

'Clarence? Did you find her?' Ava sobbed.

'Not yet…I interviewed Wallace.'

'I thought that was a dead end?'

'Not quite. You see, when you look your most innocent that is when we Detectives can tell you are up to no good.' Clarence gave a wry smile.

'I'm not following.' Ava crinkled her forehead and walked towards Clarence. 'So you think he is guilty? He has Emily?'

'I had to ask him some very personal questions, Ava. I must beg forgiveness from DI Burke for my proposition earlier.' Clarence trailed off, consumed by the reaction Burke had to Landon finding his own personal abyss. Landon had always been emotionally cold, it was a trait Ava accepted, and it wasn't new that he had hardened to the world. It made him an incredible Detective. 'I don't believe Wallace has Emily,' he answered.

'How can you be so certain?' Ava leaned in closer.

'There would be only two reasons Wallace would be involved in her disappearance; one, for his own sexual gratification, and two, to supply his connections.'

'Why are you convinced he doesn't have her?' Ava backed away. It wasn't what she wanted to hear; her little girl, surrounded by deviants.

Clarence realised he had overstepped the mark

during the interview of how he could use language as a way of speaking to perpetrators in an attempt to empathise, and the deviant terminology wasn't something he wanted to bring home.

'He wouldn't betray…again… his long term friend and in his own words, he "likes a little hair on the playing field".'

'His friend?'

'Daniel Grayson.' Clarence took his tea and lay on the sofa but Ava didn't follow.

CHAPTER 17

You shouldn't have said that

The aroma of the caramelised onions and beef sizzling in the pan was not a distant memory. Ava had always enjoyed cooking, and she had been waiting for the perfect opportunity to cook Boeuf Bourguignon. She had been watching Julia Child - The French Chef since its pilot episode, and she shared Julia's fondness for wine, neither was she afraid of the use of butter, and her daughter, Emily would always copy her closing line, "Bon appétit", before tucking into that evening's meal.

This would be the first meal Ava cooked since Emily's disappearance, and it brought home happy memories but sadness with the realisation that Emily wasn't laughing in the next room waiting for her dinner. And although Ava experimented with the more complex recipe, she tended to stick to more domestic meals as Clarence had a delicate stomach. Although he described eating as "a physical pleasure", he expressed the utmost horror when he was asked to try sushi and generally frowned on European delicacies, but tonight's casserole was not for Clarence.

The sumptuous, rich, slow-cooked beef casserole that was braised with red wine bubbled inside the oven, and Ava smiled at her accomplishment. It made the perfect stunning and comforting winter meal. She dipped her spoon into the brown sauce and tasted the hearty and flavourful, fall apart beef and slow cooked root vegetables that were enrobed in the rich red wine gravy.

The knock at the door came quietly at first, Wallace and Claudia had barely even heard it. As Wallace walked towards his front door, he found himself pleasantly surprised to see Ava standing there with a dish between her hands.

'Hello, Ava, to what do we owe the pleasure?'

'Hi, Wallace, I cooked Boeuf Bourguignon.' Ava smiled, gesturing that the dish was getting heavy.

'What's that?'

'Beef Stew,' she sighed,

'Oh righty. Oh….do come in. You can put it in the kitchen over there. Look, Claudia, Ava has brought round dinner, beef, something.'

Claudia stood up with a lost-for-words expression as she watched Ava walk towards the kitchen. 'Oh, Ava you shouldn't have…I'm so sorry about Emily.'

Ava smiled. 'I still keep hope, she's out there somewhere. We'll find her, and the pleasure was all mine. You were both so generous and understanding. Please take my offering.'

Wallace looked towards Claudia, 'What about your plans, darling?' he asked his wife.

'Oh bummer, I'm so sorry, Ava. I've already made arrangements, but do stay. I wouldn't want your hard efforts gone to waste, and besides, Wallace hasn't eaten yet. You'll be fine, darling, won't you?' Claudia pleaded to her husband.

Being left alone in the house with Ava was like Wallace's dreams come true.

Claudia had been gone for thirty minutes and Wallace had already poured the wine. Ava despised the behaviour of the lecherous more senior Wallace, but tonight she forgot her drainpipe jeans and Capri trousers and opted for an Audrey Hepburn printed short dress. Ava dressed in a way that tonight it would be part and parcel that Wallace would be staring freely at her breasts.

'This is delicious, Ava. Mind if I have a second helping?' He scoffed.

'Not at all, let me.' Ava stood taking Wallace's bowl and walked into the kitchen. She took out a small bag from her purse that contained two round white pills. After all her preparations, she felt like she had earned her reward already. She emptied the bag, tipping them onto the counter and spread them apart as if they were gold and rubbed her hands together with a devilish grin. Ava glanced over her shoulder. Her victim was swigging his wine and gleaming back at her with a slight nod. The Hendersons could play their passive aggressive horseshit games all they liked, but Ava saw straight through it. Since Emily disappeared, she meticulously planned something bad coming Wallace's way. Would it be a freak accident, an unfortunate act of bad luck such as a tyre blow-out that would send him swerving off the side of the road, or would she bash Claudia over the head and pin it on Wallace? *Decisions.*

It wasn't a need for revenge that persuaded Ava to make her next move. It wasn't a sense that gnawed at her, unceasing in its efforts; it was the need for answers.

She crushed one pill with the base of the wine bottle, scooped up the powder and stirred it into Wallace's bowl of Boeuf Bourguignon. Kidnapping wasn't on Ava's initial plan, but she knew it would be a cinch to kidnap Wallace. He'd been watching her ever since he and Claudia had moved in, and he was as gullible as a dog being tempted with a sausage. As she watched him slurp his way through his second helping and listened to him droning on about his medical grievances, conspiracy theories and personal pet aversions, all Ava could think about was shoving him into the back seat of her Vauxhall Victor.

It didn't take long before Wallace gyrated back and forth as he tried to steady himself. 'Appears I've had a bit too much to drink, Ava,' he laughed.

'I had better let you get to bed then...' Ava leant forward and placed her hand on his knee. 'Would you mind walking me home?' she suggested.

'I though' you' neva ask...' he slurred.

They stepped out into the bitter winter air. Her dress lifted and she shivered with a "whoo". Wallace stumbled along beside her and after only ten staggering steps they had reached Ava's harvest yellow Vauxhall. As he doubled over to steady himself, she lifted her hands above her head with the casserole dish between them, and she pulled her arms down sending the casserole dish crashing down onto Wallace's shoulders. He dropped to his knees and slumped over as if she had killed him; he was barely conscious and cold to the touch. Ava looked side to side, wondering at that moment if her nosey neighbours, Jane and John, had been peeking behind their curtain during that split second, but the road was empty and the houses were dark. She took the dish back inside and put it on the kitchen counter, grabbed her keys, locked the front door, and walked towards her car. As Ava opened the rear door, Wallace grunted and she bent down to reassure him he had just fallen over and she was going to seek help. By opening the other door on the opposite side, she reached across the bench seat to pull him into the car, slammed the door against his head, ran round the other side, and shoved his feet in so the other door would close. She could hear him grunting and took a deep breath whilst holding onto the steering wheel. She drove to the most isolated area that she knew – where she knew there would be some Ty-Rap cable ties waiting.

Wallace was warm enough not to be dead, but he lay so motionless that she wondered what would have happened if she gave him both pills. It took approximately three hours before Wallace came round, and when he did, he woke up inside her car. He pulled himself up and craned his neck to look out of the window, and he smelled a musty scent as he looked out into darkness.

'Good. You're awake,' Ava sighed with relief.

'What are you doing? Where are we?' He begged.

Ava stared at Wallace. He exhaled in frustration, and she stared back in silence as if debating what to do. He lowered his head, 'You think I have Emily?'

'No, I want to know what you know about Daniel.'

'Daniel? I….I don't know anything about Daniel.'

'BULLSHIT.' Ava screamed. 'I know you knew Daniel, you told Clarence, and we're going to sit here for as long as it takes for you to tell me exactly how you knew Daniel.'

Landon and Burke were working the late shift that evening at the police station. Landon rarely smiled, and he spoke in a long-winded and pedantic way that Burke often found frustrating.

They sat at opposite desks. The walls were grey, and the room had only one window. Landon's desk was neat and uncluttered. Unlike Burke's – they were like chalk and cheese.

Burke observed the fresh flowers on her desk, the only element of colour in the room. The flower vase was elegant in its simplicity and allowed the purple flowers to exude their vibrancy. As she smelled their fragrance she sighed, it had been a long time since anyone had given her flowers.

'I wish you would open up, Landon,' she pleaded as he rifled through paperwork. 'Whilst you have made me who I am today which I am very grateful for...' she continued as she fingered the petals.

'No need for expressions of recognition,' he answered.

'Look,' she said as she stood up and walked beside him stroking the side of his arm. 'I cannot imagine what you're going through.'

'It is an incomprehensible tragedy, Burke.'

Landon was aloof most of the time, and despite his manipulative abilities when it came to criminals he possessed a desire to do well; he just lacked social skills.

'Well, thank you for the flowers.'

'Flowers? Don't thank me, Burke. Bloody insect attractants.'

Inspector Atkinson tapped at the door, 'Excuse me, Landon, there's a Mrs Henderson out front quite hysterical.'

'I'm on my way,' Landon jumped out of his seat and glanced at Burke. The pair hurried down the corridor to find a distraught Mrs Henderson.

Claudia paced back and forth. She felt the need to move without pause. The anxiety coursed through her veins as she told Landon and Burke that Wallace was missing. She had the look on her face like someone had hooked her up to an electric fence and was toying with the idea of flicking the switch. Burke settled her into a seat before her panic grew. Claudia shook like a leaf in a winter's storm and was strangled by the air she breathed. 'He's gone,' she muttered.

'Perhaps he has just gone for a walk?' Burke tried to reassure her.

'No, not my Wallace, I know what he is like.' Claudia's heart raced on, and she tensed with a primal urge to get up and flee. Her eyes grew puffy and she was a shadow of her former self.

'So let's get this straight, Mrs Henderson,' Landon stated whilst clearing his throat. 'You came home early from being out with friends and discovered Wallace wasn't home? Correct?'

'Correct….'

'And this is unusual?'

'Well   no,   but   he   wasn't alone….your….wife…partner…Ava was with him.'

'What do you mean with him?'

'She had baked a beef something and dropped it round; I left them to eat as I had already arranged a prior engagement.'

Burke looked at Landon and reassured him she would stay with Mrs Henderson whilst he drove home to check on Ava.

Clarence drove home immediately and every headlamp from an oncoming car resembled a ghost charging towards him. He shuddered as he drove through the roaring winds and leant forward as water droplets splashed on his windscreen. The skies hung low like a grey blanket, and as it darkened he could barely tell the difference between sky and clouds, and after beseeching himself that everything was going to be fine he called into question his own uncertainty.

As his car came to a grinding halt outside his residence, he flung open the door and ran inside. His forehead glistened with cold sweat as he checked every room, and the hairs on the nape of his neck bristled. 'AVA? AVA,' he shouted, but no one was home.

He stood in silence with just the tap dripping into the sink; he had meant to fix it the night before. Outside there was no traffic, no birds, and he wondered if this was how Ava felt, coming home to find Emily missing. Had he got Wallace wrong? Had he now snatched Ava? And why? The house was so cold; it felt like the air would freeze there and then, and he shuddered inside his coat. As he released a slow controlled breath he saw the casserole dish on the kitchen counter. *Ava hated Wallace*, Landon thought to himself as he picked it up to smell its contents. He quickly put the dish down having realised the contents had spilled out to the sides and he rinsed his hands under the tap. But in a fleeting moment he saw his hands were red and sticky. The blood rinsed between his fingers, and as his pale hands came to light he collapsed onto his knees. Sickness enveloped him as the stains etched themselves into his mind.

Landon had blood on his hands. He saw it as a symbol of guilt, and as in Macbeth, there was enough blood on his hands to turn the entire sea red. He couldn't protect Emily, and he couldn't protect Ava.

CHAPTER 18

Missing

Most people are fortunate and their children are found relatively quickly, but for others it can be a paralysing moment of uncertainty; when hope and fear fight against one another. Clarence was in this trap. He heard the stories and he thought: *what if it was my family?* It never occurred to him it would come true.

Clarence discounted the possibility Emily had run away from home, and at the time of her disappearance she had few personal possessions beyond her pyjamas and a teddy bear named Jenkins.

Tenley Burke knocked at the front door and Clarence dragged himself to answer it. Every knock seemed louder than the first, and he felt himself losing control. As he opened the door, she stood there gawping.

'Are you all right, Landon?' she asked as she walked inside. She followed Landon towards the kitchen and she wrinkled her forehead with worry. 'Is that blood?'

Landon ignored the question. 'For Christ's sake, Landon, answer me.'

He hesitated and then said, 'Yes. I think it's Ava's.'

Burke didn't respond. Her unspoken words were somehow more clear than if she had replied.

'What are you thinking, Burke?'

'Just one thing is bothering me.'

'What?'

'Why did she cook for Wallace?' Burke asked.

'I'm still trying to figure that one out myself.'

'What, the great Detective Landon can't see it?' she said disbelievingly.

He looked at her with his head tilted to one side.

'Are you saying I am emotionally compromised?'

'OK, listen to me for a moment. Consider this. Ava cooked Wallace a meal to seduce him. After all, a way to a man's heart is through his stomach.'

'Not technically….' Landon began.

'Has the fat lady sung?'

'We don't know what Ava was thinking or feeling. I'm not going to make that assumption, not at this point anyway.'

'Landon, you're negotiating like an eighty-year-old prostitute.'

'Burke, as much as I enjoy your use of colloquialisms, I fail to see your point.'

'It was planned!' Burke walked over to the casserole dish and pointed to it, 'This was Boeuf Bourguignon. You don't eat this. Your tastes are narrow. You can't even eat two boiled eggs unless they are the same size.'

'The point being, Burke?'

'The point being, Landon, is that this would have had to be cooked for at least two hours, maybe four. It would require the freshest of ingredients; three lbs of good-quality braising steak and garden fresh vegetables like carrots and onions braised in a red burgundy.'

'Sounds positively revolting, and a waste of a perfectly good wine if you ask me.'

'Is there anything in foreign cuisine that you like, Landon?' Burke huffed.

'Of course, but I don't see why you have to mix every ingredient under the sun. Just enjoy it for what it is, and I like to see what I'm eating.'

'And this knife, no way would you have left this carelessly out in the open. If Ava did indeed plan to kidnap Wallace, and I'm not saying that is the case but humour me for a moment. If she did, she would have wanted to execute it flawlessly. Wallace is a big guy; it would have to be a sure thing if she was to have succeeded. Besides, if it was the other way round, why would Wallace return the casserole dish in your kitchen and then steal Ava's car? What time did you leave for work this morning?'

'It was early, not sure exactly…1:04 am.'

'Right, the late shift…' Burke paced up and down tapping her lips with her fingers. 'So, Ava gets up and decides she wants to kidnap Wallace, then what?'

'Goes shopping?'

'Bingo. Butchers, greengrocers, wine…'

'Ava doesn't use greengrocers, she grows her own vegetables. She has an allotment.'

'When was the last time you went there?'

'When we first met; she tried to convince me it was a rewarding activity, but it is insupportable to want to simply flicker off the soil and eat the food there and then,' he murmured.

'Ah yes your OCD… of course, I almost forgot your aversion to dirt.' Burke laughed, but he frowned, unable to see the amusement.

CHAPTER 19

Tell the truth or eventually someone will tell it for you.

The dark night was thick and the torch Landon carried in his right hand gave hardly any visibility along the path he and Burke took as they abandoned the Bristol. They walked towards Ava's allotment under the dark vastness of the night. The stars lit the sky like snowflakes, and Burke felt the wind tousle her hair as they ventured nearer. At most, they could see at arm's length, and the biting wind chill snapped at them, raising hairs along their arms. Landon's blood ran cold. They bowed their heads as they drew nearer, and although the air temperature was cool, Landon was sweating; he could feel it seeping down his spine and damping the top of his trousers.

When they were fifty yards away, they could hear the faint screams of someone in the distance. Burke pulled closed her coat and tucked her chin downwards, her breath offering a moment of warmth to her face, and they quickened their pace. Neither Burke nor Landon knew what to expect. Landon feared the worst; that Ava had been kidnapped by Wallace, and he had done it right under Landon's nose. He remembered what Ava had told him when she voiced her concerns, "There is something off about Wallace"…and he stopped then pulled Burke under the refuge of a tree.

'What's wrong, Landon?'

'Hear me out. What if Wallace has killed her? She said he was a "bit off".'

'What? Like Gorgonzola?' Landon, trust me on this one. Wallace hasn't killed Ava.'

As Burke grabbed onto her sidearm, Landon panicked.

'Not yet...' he pleaded as he grabbed her arm.

'Not this again, Landon. That was a long time ago, you don't need to panic this time. I'm not sure why back then you overreacted so much,' she dismissed.

'Because you fucking shot me, that's why!' he grunted.

'I've already apologised for that. Besides I don't carry that 9mm Short anymore. A butterfly could have farted in another country and that thing would have gone off.'

'You should have stuck with the tear gas.'

'Let's not go over old ground shall we, Clarence.'

Landon's mind twisted with anxiety. As they approached the Vauxhall, Landon ran his hand along the paintwork, and then looked out towards the shed. Burke ran towards the shed drawing her side-arm.

'Stay here,' she demanded as she scoped the area.

The shed was a deep hue of brown, and Landon wondered what they would find inside. The frosted windows were shuttered and the vegetable patch had ghostly peat mounds among the overgrown garden.

As Landon scouted the surrounding area for any signs of Ava or Wallace, a smell assaulted his nose. Decomp.

His stomach turned somersaults. Landon could hear Burke trying the door to the shed. It was locked.

'Someone's inside, Landon,' she yelled. The locked door kept whoever was inside from escaping, but Landon's nose fidgeted from the smell. He could not remember ever encountering that particular smell, but he imagined it akin to rotten eggs. With the nauseating stew of odours combined with the sharp hit of ammonia, Landon knew it was the gasses of hydrogen sulphide. Trying to ignore the odours, he saw a figure kneeling motionless on the ground. 'THIS IS THE POLICE DO NOT MOVE!' he yelled whilst pointing his gun at the shadowy figure. It didn't move. The night had a bite of frost and Landon breathed in the cold air faster, he stepped cautiously along the fallen leaves and paused when the figure became more visible.

'Ava?' he asked whilst still pointing his gun. In that suspended moment his heart stopped, and he looked along the barrel of the Browning Hi-Power Mark 1, conflicted that he was pointing a gun at Ava. 'Nod if you're OK,' he asked, lifting his eyes to see where Burke was.

Ava nodded. Tears began to run down her face.

'Where's Wallace, is he inside the shed?'

'Yes,' she mumbled.

Landon could hear Burke shouting something inaudible, but as he kept the gun aimed at Ava, Burke appeared with Wallace; he was bruised and bloodied, but he was alive. As they walked towards Landon, Wallace appeared terrified; he looked at Ava with genuine fear and struggled to free himself from the cuffs behind his back.

'Help me,' he pleaded.

'Shut up,' Burke answered.

Burke gestured to Landon to take Wallace so she could secure Ava. As he lowered his gun, Wallace ran towards him. 'You've got to get me out of here, she's crazy!' he screamed. Landon reared back his arm that held his gun and struck Wallace across the face with the back of his hand.

'Burke told you to shut up, you do not have to say

anything, but it may harm your defence if you do not mention when questioned, something which you later rely on in court. Anything you do say may be given in evidence.'

Burke pulled Ava to her feet. 'You too, Sunshine. Let's get going.'

Superintendent Floyd had allowed Landon a lot of slack over the last few years believing in the importance of the work he was doing, and Floyd had turned down a much more prestigious job to do so; Landon respected him for it. He had always promised Landon that whatever resources he needed he would provide, but he also needed DI Tenley Burke to keep him in check.

Floyd had been displeased to learn of the recent arrest, his no nonsense attitude often clashed with that of Landon, but he did have one common goal and that was becoming more progressive towards investigating murders with behavioural studies, and he knew the importance of Landon's creative acts of extracting confessions.

'Sir,' Burke approached Floyd, 'we've held Wallace Henderson for nearly three hours, we need to speak to him before he calls a lawyer.'

'Burke, how is he?' Floyd asked.

'Henderson?'

'No, Landon.'

'As cock-sure as ever, Sir,' she replied.

'He's back then?' Floyd laughed.

'He didn't go anywhere, Sir.'

Floyd paced his office, 'Get Landon in there, but keep an eye out.'

'Understood.'

Landon sat down at the table in the interview room, and as he did so Wallace smiled.

'Appears we have gone full circle, Clarence.'

'Coffee?' Landon asked.

'No, thank you,'

Landon leaned back and looked at Burke who was standing behind him and asked for a coffee.

'I'm going to ask you a series of questions, and I want you to be truthful,' Landon stated for the record.

'There has been a misunderstanding…'

'Please just stick to answering my questions. Can you do that?'

Wallace nodded.

'Your record looks clean apart from the Arden Brokers scam and your contacts. Says here that you grew up in Bromley? What brought you to Harlow?' Landon licked his finger as he flipped the pages within the folder.

'Work,' Wallace's answers were short.

'So you know your way around, short cuts, back roads, wooded areas?'

'I guess so…'

'What are you doing for work?'

'Retired.'

'Hobbies?' Landon probed.

'Erm…' As Wallace looked towards the ceiling, Landon withdrew some items from under the table and placed them in front of Wallace.

'You see, Wallace, when your wife came to the station declaring you as a missing person, our lab technicians conducted a search of your house. We found this,' Landon pointed to a piece of paper and Wallace leaned forward.

'I'm sorry,' Wallace began to tear.

'I'm sure you are, but you need to tell us for what.' Landon's patience was wearing thin.

'I never hurt anyone, I swear. I want a lawyer.'

Burke cleared her throat and called Landon outside. 'Go home, Clarence, shower, eat. You're no good to anyone after thirty-six hours, he's not going anywhere. He won't speak, he has no intention.'

'He's a narcissist, Burke; he thinks he's smarter than everyone.'

'So what was his motivation? It's not sexual.'

'Let's go find out.'

As Burke walked back into the room and towards Wallace, she collected the piece of paper on the table, As Atkinson walked him out she looked at the note in her hand. It was Ava's routine.

'Burke, are you coming?' Landon asked.

'Where?'

'Ava.'

Ava didn't fit the profile of who had abducted Emily, and Landon stood outside the room where Ava was held. He saw her jerking and panicking trying to loosen her hand restraints that kept her arms on top of the table. The cold metal dug into her skin, and she clenched her teeth as they sliced through flesh. The door opened and slammed shut behind Landon and Burke, making her jump with the slight slack she had.

'Ava Willows?' asked Burke. Landon stayed quiet. 'I'm here to ask you a few questions, do you understand?' Ava nodded slowly and looked at Landon. 'Can you confirm your name for the record? I'm going to press record now.'

Landon positioned himself into the chair opposite. Ava hadn't answered right away, and it irritated Burke. 'Name,' she asked sternly.

'Ava Willows.'

'Can you tell us what you were doing at the allotment?' Burke was ready to take down notes.

'This will go a lot quicker if you answer.'

'I told him to shut up,' Ava replied.

'Wallace? Why?'

'He was singing like a canary,' Ava shrugged.

Landon leaned forward, 'Did he shut up?' Burke looked at Landon, 'What do you mean singing?'

Landon answered for Ava, 'If he sang like a canary then he simply did what the bird naturally does, sing; an idiom for informing against someone to the police or other authority about their criminal or illicit behaviour. Wallace had already squealed to Scotland Yard, I doubt anyone would put it past him to do it again.'

Ava nodded. 'He did what I asked.'

'Then why torture him?' Burke queried.

'Because I wanted to,'

'That's not good enough. Do you have information regarding the disappearance of your daughter, Ava?' Burke pushed further.

The bare bulb in the interview room swung gently above their heads, and Landon sat with his hands cupped in his lap.

'They all bought your story, didn't they, Ava? Even I did.'

'Especially you, Clarence,' she answered.

'Where's Emily?'

'I told you before, I don't know,' Ava pleaded.

Landon stood slamming the table with his fist.

'Damn it, Ava! Then why Wallace? He was beaten black and blue.'

'He's a bad guy.'

'Why was he watching your routine? Why was he taking notes of your routine?'

'He's obsessed with me. I told you that before.'

Burke stopped the recording. 'Landon, a word outside.'

Landon became frustrated, if anyone could avoid his tactics it was Ava. His questions were fired too quickly, she had an answer for every question, and he failed to see the persona beneath her veneer. Burke and Landon viewed Ava behind the one-way glass window. She swayed side to side almost in sync with the bulb.

'Do you think Ava took Emily, Landon?'

'No, I don't know anymore. These people, Ava, aren't monsters we can just see on the street, they're regular people like you and I. I don't think I can do this.'

'Landon, if anyone can break her it's you. You know her better than anyone, and you are the best damn cop I know. She might be calling the shots right now, but you've got to look past who she is and do your job.'

Landon always appreciated Burke's kick-up-the-butt approach. It was just what he needed to see past who was in the room.

The interview room smelled like body odour. Landon had learnt to not only trust his eyes but also his sense of smell. It wasn't always his visual impressions that played a part in assessing a subject. He knew Ava had recently bathed, and he could smell the Caleche by Hermès, a Floral Aldehyde fragrance he had bought her some months before, and he could see a bead of sweat forming on her upper lip where her autonomic nervous system was working overtime. He knew how Ava normally behaved, so he noticed the subtle signs of deception; her facial expressions, speech patterns, and body language. Ava changed her head position quickly when he asked her why she was at the allotment. Of course he didn't expect the truth, and he wasn't really listening. Her head bowed down as she answered, and it told Landon she was about to lie. Her breathing accelerated and her voice became shallow – her heart rate and blood flow had changed because she was feeling nervous, because she was lying.

Ava tried to validate her lies by repeating them, and Landon noticed she shuffled her feet, something she did when he caught her up to no good at home like eating an extra slice of cake when she told him she hadn't. He smiled briefly at the memory.

CHAPTER 20

Some things are best left buried

Clarence wasn't interested at this point in time whether Ava's confession would be accepted as evidence by a court. He wanted to find Emily.

'You see, Ava; truth has a habit of unveiling itself.'

'You are not always right, Clarence,' she smirked.

'But I am. I am always right. It is so unvarying it's disconcerting,' Clarence retorted.

'You sit there with your bow tie and your grandiloquent name...' she started.

'That's a big word for you, Ava...grandiloquent.'

'I'm not going to tell you anything, Clarence,' she sneered.

'Your presence at the allotment cries your culpability, Ava.'

'This is your moment isn't it, your moment of theatre? Your idiosyncrasies and silly moustache don't work on me,' she shrugged.

'My moustache is magnificent and you know it. But this isn't about me nor my king-stache. This is about Emily. Don't you *want* to find her?'

'She's dead! She's dead! Dead, Clarence!'

Clarence stood up and walked out of the room. His insides started to die slowly at the toxicity of her words. It just needed a light and he was done. His heart pounded louder and louder as time stood still. He looked through the window and stared at Ava who sat motionless with her hands on the table. He still had a job to do, and that was to find Emily, dead or alive.

He recalled one of the last bodies he found; the victim had been discovered by a local dog walker. The body, a woman in her late thirties, was face down with her arms outstretched and bent at the elbows. Clarence remembered attending the scene and establishing she had been in the water, which had slowed decomposition, for at least two days. She hadn't endured any facial mutilation and appeared quite wax-work like. It led to an investigation that helped find other women; that's when the circus started. Clarence had been at the scene most of the day. There were several police vehicles, and it provided relief when they took her away, knowing she was now safe and dry.

DI Burke would easily say Landon was emotionally constipated, and she described that particular event as one of the craziest times in her career, but Landon said it didn't even make his top ten.

Whilst Clarence was emotionally rigid with Ava's confession, DI Burke was following an inquiry back in Harlow. The fact that less than three per cent of children are abducted by strangers gave Clarence some comfort in finding the perp, but he doubted whether he could ever accept Emily was dead. If the press found out about Ava's confession, it would be reasonable to believe that although death brings a sense of finality and closure, it also meant the public would stop looking.

With nothing left to lose, Clarence wanted to see Wallace. It had to be the reason Ava kidnapped him; he was the one to have killed Emily, and Clarence wanted to know where she was.

Surrounded by four grey walls, Wallace had nothing else to do but stare and look at the peeling paint and gouges in the plaster. He would do or say anything to stop himself going mad and theorising preposterous scenarios of what could have caused the holes in the wall. He looked up when he heard Clarence's mincing gait as he approached his cell.

'Clarence, you look as if you have a penny in the crack of your bottom and you're trying not to let it drop,' he sniggered.

'Wallace, come here, please,' Clarence asked as he gestured Wallace towards the bars that separated them. The lights flickered in the hallway above them, and a faint drip of water in the distance from an old water pipe offered the only sound; they were alone. As Wallace sauntered towards the DCI, Clarence remained motionless, and as he was inches away Clarence reached out for Wallace's shirt and slammed him against the bars.

'We're going to have that conversation again, Wallace…where's Emily?'

'I could tell you, Clarence, but you would never believe me,' Wallace sniggered.

'Try me,' Clarence snarled. Wallace smiled.

'There were two in the bed and the little one said, roll over, so they both rolled over, and one fell out, and that fucker's you!' Wallace sang.

'Let's cut through the shit shall we, Wallace.'

'You know what it is, Clarence? It's cutting through the shit and saying what is in the room, and if that is rude, well, I'm fucking sorry, but I'm having a good time and I invite you to do the same.'

Clarence wasn't known for his patience, and Wallace tested the very limits of how far Clarence could be pushed. There was only one other case that infuriated Landon. Another case that involved an innocent child; it was a couple of years ago on the 23rd of April, 1968, and news hit that a body of a young boy had been found outside the gates of Cherkley Court in Mickleham, Surrey. He had been strangled and sexually abused. The boy was identified as Roy Tutil, a fourteen year old who had been murdered on his way home from school. The only information police had was that a bus driver had seen him talking to a driver described as a "short, stocky man with white hair" in a grey Austin Westminster Mark II car. Scotland Yard and DCI Landon had been called in to assist in the investigation, but no evidence other than the suspect being "A" or "O" blood group had been found. Clarence felt the suspect was a repeat offender and it wasn't a random act, and although he regularly reviewed the file, the only thing he had to go on was the boy hitchhiked to save money for a new bicycle and had been found dumped three days later. It happened no more than an hour from Clarence's home town, and it took a toll on his mental health. It was one of the last cases Burke and he worked together. Emily's disappearance brought it all back. But Landon's anger wouldn't find Emily, and if he let himself show emotion, then people like Wallace would see it and prey upon it. It's what these types of people did. *How can I be patient when time is running out?*

'I'm not having a good time, Wallace. Just tell me what I need to know.'

'Then we're going to have to start from the beginning.'

CHAPTER 21

Black Widow

Ava Willows was born on Friday, March 2nd, 1936, just another child born to terraced houses in a poor working class area of south-east England. In the 1930s, the economy was struck by depression. At the start of 1933, unemployment was at 22% and fell substantially, falling to 13% when Ava was born. Mr and Mrs Willows found bringing up a child during pre-war Britain too difficult, and sent Ava off at just three years of age to live at a foster home, although Ava was the only child to Bob and Maureen Willows. Everybody knew everybody, Ava went to the same school as all her friends and despite the hardships, it was a supportive, loving community.

She went to the local state school only marginally failing her eleven plus. As the late 40s approached, Ava became heavily involved in a vanguard youth culture, where she was culturally savvy and socially conscious. Rock 'n' Roll was there, and The Beatles were everywhere. She wore thick black make-up, her hair got blonder, and she idolised Dusty Springfield. She had big curls in her hair, the skirts eventually became shorter, and she stayed in-tune with the latest fashion trends.

She developed a friendship with someone from the opposite sex, a boy called Andy Walters, and Ava was quite taken by the idea that he had the same initials as her; AW. They used to go everywhere and do everything together, and she would look after him as if she was an older sister much like she had whilst in the foster home, and she was convinced she had made a life-long friend.

One sunny morning, he invited her to join him at the local train tracks. She was unable to go, and tragically Andy died. According to a witness, Andy and other friends were playing near the tracks. All of a sudden there was a flurry of exhilaration, and a couple of children ran around shouting, "I can't see him". Two policemen came running towards the commotion, but it was too late. They confirmed someone had fallen onto the live track. Ava was devastated, and she visited his parents often. She blamed herself, but she always blamed everyone else, too. It wasn't long after Andy's death that Ava left school, and at just eighteen years old she became engaged to a local boy. Her apparent satisfaction of ordinary life wasn't to last long. All the girls around Ava aspired to the classic husband and two children, and part of her wanted that too, but being brought up in a foster home with a sense of self importance, Ava wanted more from life, and two kids and marriage would not be as stimulating as what Ava would envision. For her, she required a certain amount of violence, a somewhat S&M quality to her relationships. The role of dominant and submissive, she had to know her role.

She landed a secretarial job at a soap manufacturer where she ultimately met her husband-to-be, Daniel Grayson. Daniel Grayson was described as extremely good looking, aloof, well-dressed, who used to have a big motorcycle that everyone wanted to have a ride on. Ava was mesmerised. To say Ava had become absolutely fascinated by Daniel would be an understatement; after all, there weren't many motorcycles around. It wasn't until the New Year's Party that they got together and became an item. From then on, Daniel became indoctrinated into her views on politics, sex, religion and so forth.

With no mother and father figure to speak of during her crucial years, with her "I'm too good for this job position" attitude, she worked menial jobs before securing her position at the soap manufacturer. Her obsession with the Second World War had been well documented during her stay at the foster home. Even though she spent the majority of her childhood alone, conversations among the other children often revolved around Nazis. When she met Daniel, she believed he embodied everything she desired in a man, of course, at this time he was unaware of her lurid fascinations. Other men were dull and un-ambitious, and for Daniel, Ava was enigmatic and worldly. He had no idea she emulated the archetypal Aryan image of blonde hair and blue eyes, but it was only the beginning to what became the start of a twisted and tumultuous relationship.

Clarence couldn't believe what he was hearing. According to Wallace, Ava wanted a life on the edge.

'I'm sorry, Wallace, this all seems very far-fetched.'

'I haven't even got to the good part yet, Clarence.'

Wallace's story continued. Daniel became totally besotted with Ava. He'd soak up all her distorted philosophical ideologies, and that was when Wallace became concerned for his friend. He'd shout for Daniel, and he'd completely ignore him. Daniel became involved in her sadomasochistic deviancies, and his personality became fused more and more to that of Ava.

It wasn't long before Ava's past caught up with

her. Hearsay claimed that she had been convicted of murdering her first fiancé, Michael, known by his friends as Mini-Mike, but how much of that is true Wallace didn't know. It was then when cracks started to appear in her relationship with Daniel.

'What exactly had she been accused of, Wallace?'

'Look, Clarence, I'm only tellin' you what I know. Don't shoot the messenger,' Wallace held up his hands in defence.

'I'm listening,' Clarence whispered.

'I'll spare the gory details.'

'Don't!' Clarence demanded.

No one had ever heard of Ava Willows, not in this part of the country anyway, and that was probably concluded because what she had been accused of doing was apparently so gruesome that nobody wanted to cover the gory details. The fact that newspapers wouldn't publish it and the media kept it off air, allowed Ava to try and start a new life – with Daniel.

But when someone recognised her in the street, they had to make a decision as to whether the story would be palpable for people to read whilst eating breakfast, and the decision was no, it couldn't. So horrific was the crime, it's told that anyone who viewed the evidence would be forever damaged.

'You're making her out to be Satan's Sister.'

'Trust me, Clarence, if any of this is true...you wouldn't be surprised to see horns growing out of her head,' Wallace shook his head.

'So regardless of this hearsay crime, what happened next?'

When Emily was born, Ava's temper became more and more wild. Her violence would usually connect to her morbid fascination with blades. Often it would become so unbearable Daniel would walk out. But he couldn't leave the child, not at such a young age. Daniel tolerated Ava; she always had dinner on the table, and knew the little things that would keep a man happy. But like her previous engagement, he, too, discovered her secret – a psychological illness. He just couldn't take the tremendous mood swings that would turn their relationship from lovers to fighters. And he hated that Emily heard them fighting.

Daniel held out for nine years, a mighty feat, and he was a self confessed expert at weathering the Ava Hurricane. At heart, he knew he loved her, but he never assumed that one day it would consume him. Clarence couldn't believe the inconceivable story Wallace was telling.

Wallace continued by saying, 'I warned Daniel, I told him, *that* one was feisty, and he should watch his back. Of course, I'd never met her before; she didn't know who I was. I just feared for him from the stories he was telling me. Like I said, this is just from what I was told. Daniel wanted out, and he wanted Emily too.' Clarence could see that Daniel just wanted a simple separation. Willows was a pleasant girl at times, and nice and friendly when she was in a good mood. Wallace had learnt by his recent ordeal to keep away when she wasn't.

Ava's mother, Maureen, went on to have another child with her husband, Bob, but when she had had enough of his drinking, gambling, and abuse, she left him for another man. Ava's mother reportedly suffered multiple black eyes from Bob, but not once did she ever reach out to Ava, and Ava never bothered back. Knowing her mother was being beaten black and blue made Ava eventually desensitised to such acts of violence. To her, that was just part and parcel of a relationship.

'I've never ever laid a hand on Ava!' Clarence remarked.

'I'm not saying you have, Clarence. But do remember, I'm just telling my story here. What you do with it is up to you.'

Ava Willows was not the kind of woman you'd just walk away from; she would possess you and everything you own. It would only be her sudden bouts of violence that frightened men off, that's if they got away.

'One did,' Clarence mumbled.

'Hmm...' Wallace continued to describe the disintegration of her marriage to Daniel and un-denying he once claimed Ava to be the most wonderful wife you could have ever asked for. Perfect wife, perfect mother, but the other side was only a split-second away.

'So, what happened to Daniel?' Clarence leaned forward. It was like he was hearing a horror story. It certainly didn't seem like he was talking about anyone he knew, let alone the woman he slept next to at night.

Daniel had told Ava he would be home at 9pm one evening. When the clock struck 9, Daniel still wasn't home. Preparing dinner with Daniel absent was the ultimate insult. She felt rejected, *apparently*, and the only thing that would make her feel better was to get revenge. So, when he eventually came home that evening, she was waiting for him in the kitchen. His dinner was still on the table, albeit it had a huge carving knife sticking through it, through the plate and about 2 inches deep into the oak table. Daniel chose not to involve the police, but from that night on, this bloody carving knife had its own hook hanging in the kitchen, in full view.

'Do you think she has picarism?'

'I don't think anything, Clarence. What's that....?'

'Picarism, a sexual desire to prick someone's skin.'

'What, like with a knife?'

'Or pins, razors, anything sharp.' Clarence stated.

'Heck knows. I don't really know the bitch.'

'I ask you to watch your language.'

Police attended the home of Daniel and Ava when a neighbour rang about hearing a woman scream. Ava went ballistic, and she was sent to a psych ward. Of course, she was let out; she told a good old tale about her husband's violent tendencies, and she was scared for her and her daughter's safety. Yet ironically, Daniel was the victim of violence.

'It was the excuse he needed to leave. It didn't take her long to find herself a new lover, you.'

'I've never witnessed any of what you have described. I'm sorry, Wallace, I'm finding this story a desperate plea.' Clarence shook his head.

In a desperate effort to hang onto Daniel and persuade his return, she overdosed on pills and alcohol in a half-hearted effort to end her life. Rather than return, Daniel called the cops, and she found herself staring at the white walls of a psychiatric ward once again.

At this point in time, Ava felt sure Daniel wouldn't come home. She tried all sorts of ploys, even risking her own life, but nothing worked. She'd never previously thought to use Emily.

Clarence interrupted; he knew at this point in the story Emily was safe. What he couldn't understand was how Wallace had even fabricated this incredulous story to begin with.

'So you're trying to tell me, Clarence Landon, that the very woman whom I have been seeing for the last six months is among the 15% of killers in this country that carry out premeditated murders. Women rarely act on impulse. Women know what they're doing. They don't turn dangerous overnight. I've not known Ava to have suffered an unfortunate background of child abuse or physical neglect that may have caused this mental disorder.'

'Why do you think I was so terrified when you found me?'

'Ava does not take a malevolent pleasure in death, Wallace. There must have been some kind of misunderstanding.'

'Yeah, and nothing is ever a lady's fault. If you believe that, you're more naive than I thought, Detective.'

'This is not going to find Emily. And to be honest, Wallace, you've wasted the few precious hours of time I have in my day.'

Clarence stood up and straightened his jacket, and he ached as he walked out of the cell.

'You know, Clarence, your feet wouldn't hurt so much if you didn't insist on wearing those patent leather shoes,' Wallace laughed. 'And, Detective, if you're looking for answers, you need to go back to the allotment.'

CHAPTER 22

The decade that shook Britain

The 60's had become a decade of sex, spies, government conspiracies, and the hippie movement. The Profumo Affair captured the public's attention when Secretary of War John Profumo was discovered to be sleeping with a woman who was also having an affair with a Russian military attaché. The affair changed the relationship the press had with the government, and it was from this point onwards that the public began to seriously question their trust in politicians.

When one mentions Scotland Yard, it probably invokes the image of a foggy London street with a detective pacing up and down in a trench coat. In reality, it wasn't far off. It wasn't really to serve the city either, but the whole greater London area. And even when the Yard sent out its first plainclothes policemen in 1842, the general public opinion was that they felt uncomfortable with "spies" on the streets.

Cops in Britain suffered a bad reputation, and since the first force had been founded back in 1829, the terms Police, Violence and Corruption seemed to go together. London police even trained pickpockets to work for them during the 1850s. It was no wonder the phrase "if you want to know the time, ask a policeman" became popular. It came from their reputation of stealing watches from Victorian drunks. Burke's father had been one of these "bent coppers". Of course, no one admitted to it, but they all knew it.

He retired in the 1950s, the supposed golden era where the Daily Mail reported "a vast amount of bribery and corruption among officers attached to a West End Station". The scandal led to the closing of ranks and the odd patsy being charged, but a large number of officers began retiring. It was the best course of action before he took Tenley, who was a Detective Sergeant at the time, down with him.

Clarence's charisma, professionalism and outstanding record helped win community trust. But it wasn't uncommon to hear about several detectives conspiring with criminals, and it would take years to begin to repair the tarnished reputation Scotland Yard had acquired.

When Jack the Ripper started his killing spree between 1888 and 1891, Scotland Yard apprehended a suspect in the White Chapel vicinity. With just a pattern to go by, the Yard relied mainly on anthropometry; the measurements of human physical traits along with racial and psychological traits. Understandably more than one hundred and sixty people were identified as the White Chapel murderer, even including Lewis Caroll, the author of Alice in Wonderland.

In 1967, the Yard moved to a twenty storey building near the Houses of Parliament, and the plainclothes detectives of the Criminal Investigation Department (CID) became respected and prominent figures in the public's eye because of their investigative methods. But with the Yard's reputation in jeopardy, and the Yard's missing persons bureau far from bustling, it was the decision of Superintendent Floyd whether the small team of women would extend their services for Clarence's missing step-daughter, Emily; currently one of the most baffling cases and as of yet, the search party, Clarence, and other police officers had failed to return a single clue other than the condescending known perpetrator in the adjacent cell.

Understandably, Scotland Yard was not very forthcoming, for they would say "Children leave home for so many reasons", followed by examples, and believed that fewer parents would experience the agony of having a child go missing if only they invested time into the child's interests. But naturally Clarence knew who Emily's friends were, her favourite locations, where she'd like to play after school, what her favourite night-time drink was, her favourite food, and her favourite place to eat at.

The name Scotland Yard had become synonymous with the greatest crime of all: murder. But as time went on, Superintendent Floyd summoned detectives from the Yard to work alongside Landon and Burke to deal with this complicated case.

DCI Landon, DI Burke and Floyd organised a team of a hundred and fifty officers to scour the allotment and the surrounding areas. But had the mention of the allotment just been a red-herring by Wallace?

By now, the photograph of Emily was posted all over the country and the media began reporting sightings. One of the more credible witnesses was reported to have seen a young blonde girl walking with an older man just outside of Harlow.

Scotland Yard was still working under the assumption the child had either been kidnapped by a paedophile ring or sold for adoption, and Clarence was still hesitant to involve them fully in the details of his discussion with Wallace.

Burke and Landon travelled together in the Bristol,

arriving at the allotment a few minutes before the rest of the team. It looked seemingly no different than their last visit, albeit the weather was more forgiving.

The day had a soft filtered light, and although the sky was bright, the cloudy day offered silver hues with a promise of rain.

Clarence despised the thought of walking in mud. The very mention of the word repulsed him, and he held his nose between his fingers like a child.

'Will you stop being such a wimp, Clarence!' Tenley said as she stormed through the entrance to the allotment.

'Can you not smell that, Tenley?' Clarence whined.

'Of course I can. But if you're going to anal exhale, I plead you do it in your own company.'

'I beg your pardon,' he scoffed.

'Just fart proudly.' She laughed. 'You don't have to be smart to laugh at farts, but you have to be stupid not to.'

'That smell, Burke, is not coming from me! It was here last time. Look around for disturbed dirt.'

Landon and Burke began searching the allotment for variations in the surface of the grounds. Small mounds and depressions could indicate someone or something had been buried. The rest of the team pulled up and came to a grinding halt. Landon and Burke looked up as they steadily joined them with shovels in tow. As the team began to dig, Clarence observed the process with worrying thoughts. Burke stroked his arm reassuring him of what they might find, expecting a traumatic and convoluted experience.

'Detectives, take a look at this.' An officer remarked as he stepped out of the grave. He dug his shovel into the ground without losing sight of what he had just dug. The other officers stood in silence.

'I can't.' Clarence had his back turned towards the site, and he started to walk away.

'Clarence, look,' Tenley tugged.

CHAPTER 23

*Once caught in a lie...everything else becomes
questionable*

Ava sat in her cell staring blankly at the wall,
unaware that Clarence had been to the allotment. He
stood outside with Inspector Atkinson as he feared
during particular circumstances he'd suffer from
auditory exclusion and miss something vital during
Ava's interview. She sat in front of DI Burke with her
eyes twinkling with a benign smile, and Clarence
stared at the suspected perpetrator of one of the
country's most diabolical murders.

Burke wanted to know Ava's story from the
beginning, and Ava corroborated Wallace's version
of events right up till the point of describing how she
met her first fiancé Michael.

At this point Burke left the room. She closed the
door behind her and looked at Landon, and she
wondered if he really wanted to stick around to listen
to the rest of the story. He hadn't shared the
information he obtained from Wallace, and it wasn't
something he would own up to; living with a woman
who was driven to kill defied any comprehension, and
Clarence had no clue.

In Ava's own words, she described an inexplicably
heinous crime. She was used to using violence and
fear to intimidate people into doing exactly what she
wanted. She saw it done in her own family whilst
growing up, and she was carrying on the tradition.
Clarence could see Ava was amused by Burke's fear,
and he'd seen her smile as she said, "Michael was

dead the moment he met me". Clarence could see Ava found the shock and distress it caused DI Burke funny. Wallace hadn't gone into detail about the so-called crime, but he feared Ava wanted to share it. *Did he want to hear it? Was it relevant to poor Emily?*

A report at the time stated that friends of Michael claimed Ava used to beat him, perhaps he beat her. It was inconclusive. There were scars on his body where she had stabbed and hit him. But when Michael told her he was only in the relationship for the sex and she had better get used to it, it wasn't the outcome Ava was after. She wanted to marry Michael, and he didn't want to marry her. Ava started to secretly keep a record of Michael's whereabouts and presented the evidence to his boss that inevitably got him fired. She told friends that if he took her back now, it would be until death do we part. He hadn't known that the fact would come sooner rather than later. But he took her back.

A few months later, Ava was desperate to hold onto Michael. Michael was desperate to get away. Friends of Michael stated in the report that after a few weeks at his new job, he showed them his scars of where Ava had tried to harm him, but he had no idea he was already two thirds into the last day of his life. They pleaded with him not to go home that evening, but while he was preparing to leave home, Ava was preparing to carry out her act of fantasy.

Ava showered, slipped on her newly purchased Baby Doll peignoir set she had bought that day, and went to bed. They had sex and then she struck. When Michael didn't show up for work the following morning, his workmates became worried. It wasn't like him to not show up; it was completely out of character. He had predicted his own death. Days prior, he had been running around town trying to get help, but no one really believed him.

When police forced their way into the home of Ava and Michael, they found her asleep on the bed. She was alive but unconscious, an array of pills lay beside her, and she was immediately taken to hospital.

Anyone that went into that house would be scarred forever. Ava Willows had stabbed Michael twenty-five times before skinning and dismembering his corpse. She then proceeded to cook parts of his body in a large pot with various vegetables.

It didn't take long for the unfathomable news to spread, and for the next week, Ava stayed in the hospital. Her testimony claimed that she stabbed him in self-defense and then lost consciousness. The Detective Sergeant at the time explained that she looked like the most ordinary woman, and due to lack of evidence, all they could charge her with was the possibility she had tampered with a body. She was admitted to a psychiatric hospital, but she got out. A few weeks later she met Daniel.

CHAPTER 24

Someone is digging your grave right now

It was clear Ava had gone undetected for so long because she was so devious in her planning. Clarence was shocked by it all. When he had visited Ava's cell, she sat in the corner in the pre-natal position looking utterly dejected and broken. He looked at Ava, and he was fascinated by the psychology of what had unfolded.

As Burke probed further, Ava discussed her relationship with Daniel. The push and pull followed by fear and paranoia.

'Ava, we know your secret.' Burke didn't know anything, not really, but she had a great poker face. Clarence viewed from behind the one-way window as he waited anxiously for Ava's answer. He desperately wanted Burke to admit that Wallace had been released, and as Ava readjusted her position, he opened the door unable to contain himself.

He sat down not saying a word.

'I don't have any secrets,' Ava retorted.

Clarence stepped in, 'Wallace has been released.'

'NO!' she gasped. 'He killed my baby!' she screamed.

'And yet you're the one with the grave, Ava.' DI Burke remarked.

'I can explain.' Ava's eyes widened and she sat firmly in her seat.

According to Ava, Daniel gave her only apathy after the daughter was born. She blamed everything on Daniel. He showed no soul, no vulnerability, instead she saw nothing. When Daniel came home late one evening, she accused him of cheating. She felt the intensity rise in her tone, and while their daughter slept, he came towards her. She feared for her life, reached for a skillet, and used it to cave in the side of his head. There was so much blood. He went down like a sack of spuds.

It explained why Ava was adamant the father was out of the picture, and Clarence wasn't to go investigating Daniel's whereabouts. She *did* have a secret, and she would do anything to keep it.

Daniel lay on the kitchen floor motionless. He lacked the spark that made a person a living being. She nudged him with her foot, but he lay lifeless. His face planted against the floor. The last thing she wanted was Emily to come downstairs and find her father lying lifeless on the kitchen tiles. Ava had to move quickly, and she had to dispose of the body. It took her over an hour to drag Daniel to her car and haul him inside; even longer to dig a grave. Thankfully, it was dark, and few people were out and about at that ungodly hour. As she patted the earth down, she wiped her forehead of the sweat beads that trickled down her face. It brought a sigh of relief that not only was Daniel and his lack of emotion now out of the picture, but she and Emily could move on. But with Daniel dead she would have to explain it gently to Emily about her father's absence. His leaving town with some floozy seemed a more appropriate answer to Emily's question than Mommy killing him.

'So, Ava, you're admitting to an unlawful killing, committed with intent to cause serious injury, where you were aware that your conduct involved a serious risk of causing death?' DI Burke questioned.

'Yes, I guess I am,' she answered.

'So where's Emily?' Clarence asked again.

'I told you. I don't know. That bastard pervert, Wallace, he took her!'

'You see, Ava, there's just a few discrepancies in your story. There's no evidence to suggest Wallace took Emily.' Clarence shook his head side to side.

'And I told you, he left during the dinner. That's when he must have taken her.'

'Then how did he get inside the house? I'm presuming you locked the front door!' Clarence stated.

'Of course...'

'And taken her where?' Clarence sighed in frustration. Ava was lying.

'That's your job, Clarence. Your fucking job. And you can't even do that right.'

Landon looked at his lap in frustration as Burke gestured they leave the room. As the door closed behind them, they both looked at Ava from the one-way window.

'Do you think Wallace took Emily, Clarence?'

'No, no I don't.'

'Do you think he's even involved?' she beckoned.

'Yes.'

'But how?'

'I don't know, but I'm bloody well going to find out. The truth is out there.'

'But so are the untruths.'

CHAPTER 25

He wore guilt like shackles on his feet

It was the morning of that dreadful day that Emily disappeared. Wallace and his pretty but dim wife, Claudia Henderson had recently moved into the neighbourhood, and they were keen to impress their new neighbours. John and Jane from across the road had bumped into Claudia when she was out front tending to her new garden. Although with a mission in mind, Claudia felt it rude not to invite them over that evening for dinner, even though she had been unimpressed by Jane's advice on how to care for her Carpathians.

Wallace and Claudia had argued all day, as usual; it grew from nowhere and escalated into rage. The move from Harlow, Claudia's home town, struck a nerve, and she had grown tired of the manipulation she had to endure because of Wallace's bad choices.

With her pruners in hand, Claudia tugged at the weeds, and her knees dug further into the soil as she pulled. Dirt under her nails wasn't something she was used to, and as she sobbed and wiped her face with the back of her hand, she saw her husband pull up on the driveway with that evening's shopping. Wallace had set his eyes on Ava as he pulled up; he smiled gently and encouraged his wife to invite her to join them that evening.

'We've just got to get through this one last time, Claudia. I promise,' he assured.

The evening couldn't have gone any better. Music escaped from every open window, and the

Hendersons hadn't been worried about pissing off the neighbours because they were enjoying it just as much. Claudia and Wallace exchanged glances from across the table during the course of the evening, and Claudia maintained the exceptional hostess role and made sure the wine was flowing.

At 21:00, Wallace dabbed his mouth and asked to be excused as he walked towards the kitchen and gave a slight nod towards his wife.

Guilt wasn't something Wallace ever felt, but it could be argued that guilt danced with greed. He ruffled his hair as he breathed in picking up the phone. Wallace needed an out, and although he knew in the long run it was the right thing to do, he couldn't help but wonder if he really was doing the right thing. *Know what your mission is, Wallace, and you will always have a purpose. It's not the money that is the issue here; it's what is right and wrong.*

He looked out from the kitchen watching Ava read a note in her lap, and he smiled as he watched her face light up. He allowed his eyes to slide over her body, calculating the pluses and minuses about her like an equation. She ranked high in his expectations, at least a nine. He wondered what she was smiling at, and as he remembered why she was there, his mouth became a straight line, the sparkle in his eyes diminished, and he gulped hard into the phone as he held it against his ear. He stroked the hair behind his ear and his insides went cold. *This wasn't right.* What he was about to do wasn't right. As he received the kidnapper's word, he hung up. The deed was done. Soon Emily was going to be taken.

CHAPTER 26

Debt free

Hearing Ava's scream sent chills down Claudia's back. And in that moment anger protected her from Ava's pain; anger towards her husband. But Ava's sadness meant the Henderson's freedom. Claudia let out a slow controlled breath.

'What now?' she asked Wallace.

'Now we just wait and do as we're told. It will all go away; we've just got to stick to our story.'

As time progressed, Ava's pain worsened. Claudia attempted to loosen her body movements, but she never was a good liar and every day became like clockwork. She rolled her head, slackening it side to side and it fooled the casual observer, but for someone with a keen eye, like Clarence, she was a walking advert for guilt.

'I can't do this for much longer, Wallace,' she pleaded.

'Yes, you can.'

'But when DCI Landon stormed through the door, I thought it was all over,' she quivered.

'They don't have anything on us. Remember, it's for the best.' Wallace nodded.

'We can't carry on like this. You did as you were asked. Let's go back to Harlow, let's go home.'

'We can't, not yet. Suspicion would fall right on us.' Wallace shook his head.

'But you said yourself; the police have nothing on us.'

'It's not part of the plan, Claudia.'

The Plan to take Emily, had played out nicely, and although Claudia felt anxious, it was because something important was on the line. Wallace had served his time. Claudia hadn't planned on returning to crime or the lifestyle of a criminal. She couldn't really see any other way out and knew anxiety was turning into paranoia. It would take her a while to learn the difference and remain calm within.

Truth prevailed after she dolled herself up for a night out with the girls; begrudgingly leaving her husband Wallace and Ava in the same room together, and it pissed her off that she had to pretend she was the stay-at-home-and-bake little housewife that made her own marmalade. *"See you later, darling."*

Claudia's tears at the station were real. After Wallace's disappearance, Claudia demanded to know from her husband what she and Wallace had got themselves into, and learning the truth enabled Claudia's discomfort to lessen. Her guilt and anxiety left her with a discomfort like being hooked up to an electric fence, knowing things were awry, but now with her recent revelation, she realised the battery wasn't even connected. She could breathe.

At this point in time, the Detectives were closing in on the truth. Ava genuinely had no idea what had happened to her child, but suspicion fell on Wallace. Giving up the truth wasn't part of the plan, but neither was going to jail. Clarence Landon and Wallace Henderson hardly saw eye-to-eye, but he could see Clarence just wanted what was in the best interest of the child. Handing over the evidence against Ava was a risky procedure, given Wallace's background. It was a fifty-fifty chance as to whether it was going to be viewed as a red-herring attempt to get out of going to jail. And he was right.

CHAPTER 27

Three may keep a secret if two of them are dead.

'Clarence, I have some interesting news.'

Those were the words that came from Detective Tenley Burke once she and Clarence had a quiet moment together. Before the allotment discovery, Burke had been in Harlow investigating a lead. Landon was learning about Ava's past, and Burke was digging further into the Henderson's. Coming straight back from Harlow, Burke knew Landon wouldn't believe what she had to say; Landon never did.   He was a I-have-to-see-it-with-my-own-eyes kind of guy. And whilst she was keen to unveil the truth, she knew no secret this grand could remain hidden forever. This type of secret would wait patiently in the dark, and slowly but surely it would manifest into something that when it blows, everything would crumble. That's how it remains intact until destiny chooses the time for it to be revealed.

The allotment discovery had gone precisely how Burke imagined. But Burke knew how the conversation with Landon would go if she revealed her findings this soon.

"You must be lying!" he would say.

"Please, Clarence, you forget yourself."

"Landon can't possibly be wrong!" he would state.

"No one can always be right." She would answer.

"But I am, always. I am right. Although it looks like I am very much wrong, that upsets me. And I

should not be upset because I am right. I must be right because I am never wrong."

Burke closed her eyes as she envisioned the exhausting conversation that she hadn't even had with Clarence.

Ava was admitted to Broadmoor hospital. Another bleak future for the woman Clarence called his love. He knew this was it. Demeaning room searches, drugged-up patients surrounded by self-harm. His and her future as he knew it was torn away from him. Ava was facing a third of her life with serial killers, despite not being convicted of killing anyone, but accusations of attacking Daniel Grayson, although a serious offence, wasn't usually one that warranted such a long incarceration.

'What's interesting, Tenley?' Clarence asked as he nursed a cup of tea. Clarence was awash with grief. The coffee shop's tables were huddled close together, but it was part of its charm, and Clarence warmed his hands around the mug blowing in serendipitous pants.

As Tenley Burke sat down opposite a desperate Clarence Landon, she pulled out a file from within her jacket, placed it on the table and slid it towards him.

'What's this?' he frowned.

'The Hendersons.'

'What about them?' Clarence opened the folder and flicked through the pages.

Clarence spotted the anomaly in the Henderson's finances. Even with Arden Brokers now closed, Wallace Henderson found ways of cheating his way to fortune. But how did he do it? How could one man rip off and keep ripping off investors? It might sound like a shocking revelation, but this wolf was so intent on catching its prey, that he actually became prey to an even bigger predator. It was the name of the game, to move money from the client's pocket to his own, and the only thing standing in his way of doing so was a bullshit story. In this case, the Hendersons were receiving an anonymous monthly income from an account in, none other than, Harlow.

Of course, aiding in the kidnapping of a nine year old child was one way to clear a debt, but one has to live.

'Daniel Grayson?' Landon looked up at Tenley and she smiled.

'Precisely.' Tenley's smile extended from one side of her face to the other. It pleased her that Landon was impressed.

'And what about Wallace?'

'What about him? He's just the hired goon. He's going to carry on doing what he does best,' she nodded.

'Whistleblowers who go up against paedophile rings usually end up dead, Burke.'

'This is right up your street, Clarence. Not only are psychopaths building the power structure, but being a paedophile is almost like next on the list of requirements. They're more often than not given positions of power because they can be manipulated by the cabal.'

'Slow down, and keep your voice down.'

Wallace Henderson had been released, and Burke knew that, like most whistleblowers that sing about the nefarious activities of the Elite, he might very well be met with a suspicious death. Scotland Yard claimed that Wallace alleged up to five paedophile rings were operational as far as he was aware, and the dossier included names of ex-government ministers. Scotland Yard had since investigated claims of serious sexual abuse by investigating the death of four boys. "We cannot stress enough what a complicated case this is", Detective Superintendent Floyd announced. The fresh lead centered on Wallace's evidence that he witnessed a boy being strangled to death by a Member of Parliament, and this had taken place after he and the boy had been in a chauffeur-driven car to the destination.

Burke furrowed her brow. 'I just cannot fathom why he would be part of it, and then snitch on his clients.'

'Because he procures women, how did he phrase it? He "likes grass on the playing field"? I can bet somewhere dear old Wallace has a conscience and deep down doesn't want to be pulled into this kind of exploitation. He prefers the monetary kind.'

'Join me for dinner?' Burke asked. 'Don't look at me like that, Clarence. You have to eat.'

'All right then.'

'Good because I've booked El Rio.'

'Haven't the police raided that place about eleven times?' he queried.

'Yes, but narcotics were never found. The owner discourages the consumption of drugs. We'll be fine. I'll pick you up at eight, and we can continue this discussion later,' she smiled.

El Rio was a Caribbean restaurant in Notting Hill, West London, recently opened by a Trinidadian community activist and civil rights campaigner, Hank Richley. A couple of years ago the restaurant became the target for police attention and raided it eleven times which led to a protest march. It ended in violence and the arrest of six protestors. Clarence had never visited the restaurant before, it wasn't to his culinary tastes, but Burke had offered to pay, and he never liked to disappoint. When they pulled up outside, Clarence could see it was dimly lit, and as they walked through the door he noticed it was adorned with black leather furniture. Calypso music came from the speakers, and waiters and waitresses were all wearing white suits with straw hats. The owner, Hank, clearly intended it to be an up-market restaurant.

'This looks a little out of sorts, doesn't it, Burke. I mean there are still some undeveloped bomb sites from the Second World War,' Clarence stated.

'Come on, Clarence.' She tugged. 'It's one of my favourite places to go; doesn't the spicy aroma of that West Indies food wafting past you just tickle your senses? I know what you're having, Banana fritters!'

Burke and Landon were seated at a table near the window.

'What is the meaning of this, Burke?'

'Landon, you won't regret it. The purpose of my invitation is simply for you to broaden your palate and try new things.'

'Forgive me, Burke. I thought you wished for me to join you to ask my opinion, perhaps on our previous discussion.'

'Stop being suspicious.'

'I can't see this evening boding well, Burke if fritters are anything to go by. Ghastly looking things.'

'Don't tell me you have ever refused a dish because it wasn't presented well.'

'Naturally. Ava once....' Clarence cleared his throat. 'Ava once, in our early courting days, tried to serve me a plate full of mush and animal innards.' Clarence said, looking disgusted by the memory. His moustache crinkled. 'The food will be inedible,' he huffed.

'We're not here to discuss food all evening, Clarence. I'm going to order for myself and for you. Sit tight. Then we can discuss more trivial matters.'

'I'll have the Chicken Kiev. Is it Russian, Burke?'

'Yes, with garlic butter.'

'Hold the garlic.'

Burke looked at Clarence wondering if the decision to bring him along had been a good one after all and she wasn't going to order the Chicken Kiev off the children's menu either. When she returned from ordering at the bar, her smile upturned the corners of her mouth and Clarence smiled back. *Just like old times.*

'What are you smiling at?' Clarence begged.

'It's not often when a woman gets to a certain age she is complemented, Clarence.' She smiled. 'A man opened the door for me, it was nice. I believed chivalry was dead.'

Burke had intended to discuss the case, but the truth was she, for the first time in a long time, could relax even if it was just for a couple of hours, and she didn't want to take that from Clarence.

Burke was genuinely pleased to see Landon, and despite the differences in their age, they had rekindled their close friendship. Burke had never really been able to work with anyone quite like she had with Landon, even if half the time he shook his head in despair.

'Christ, Burke, what is that?' he asked as the waiter lowered the plate and looked at Clarence with consternation.

'Wait until you see what you've got!' she grinned.

'It looks like a headless Cindy.'

'Who's Cindy?'

'A plastic doll I bought Emily a few weeks ago.'

'Clarence, I had hoped to kill two birds with one stone by inviting you here tonight....'

'That would be three if you include that quail!' he laughed.

They both chuckled looking at the meal.

'I've missed this, Clarence. I've missed you.'

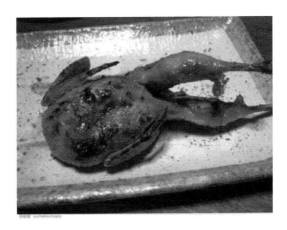

CHAPTER 28

A child's laughter could simply be one of the most beautiful sounds in the world.

The following day, Clarence stood underneath the hanging sign; a sign that once read Arden Brokers. It hung lightly against the red brick facade of the building that had high arched windows with velvet drapes, and the lace inner curtains were still drawn. There he stood. The idea that Emily could have been inside during his last visit to Harlow terrorised him because he hadn't given it a second thought; *the old Arden Broker residence.* He walked towards the entrance, and the building became monstrously enormous, but he hesitated. What would he say? If Emily was inside with Daniel, would he want to disrupt that?

Clarence imagined what would have been a beautiful rose garden was now a hostile overgrown bush, and as the wind brushed past his face he decided to sit inside his car waiting for a sign. '*This is ridiculous,*' he thought.

He buckled up, turned the engine over, and the Bristol roared. It sat idly for a few moments before he pulled away, the thought of never seeing Emily again always at the back of his mind.

The old Arden Broker residence seemed abandoned and derelict, but a playground nearby brought laughter and joy for the children playing; a gut-wrenching memory where Clarence would bask in the warm sunlight as Emily swung on swings. Her laughter echoed, and he smiled as he saw her smile.

The children ran screaming with delight, and Clarence paused. *Emily?* But it was just another intoxicated child bouncing and squealing. He sighed heavily and stroked his moustache with his finger and thumb in a downward motion as he watched the children play. He wished Burke was sitting beside him. She always knew the right thing to say.

CHAPTER 29

'Truth has only one face: That of a violent contradiction' George Bataille

Clarence looked at the girl whose blonde hair had waves of soft reflecting light. She giggled as she ran, each strand of her hair swishing in front and then away from her face. In that brief moment, in her smile and her laughter, Clarence could hear her voice like an angel. *There is nothing I wouldn't have done to keep you safe, dear Emily.* There was something intoxicating about her excitement, the way she bounced and squealed as she ran. As her grin grew wider and wider, he couldn't help but smile. He stepped out of the Bristol closing the door behind him as he approached her. 'Emily,' he shouted.

'CLARENCE!' she yelled...Emily ran faster than she had ever ran before. He bent down, opening his arms, as she drew near she lunged between them, embracing him tightly, hugging him fiercely.

'Oh I have missed you, Emily.'

'Where's mommy?' she asked.

'She's at home. What are you doing here, Emily? We've been looking for you for a very long time.'

'I'm sorry, Clarence,' the girl apologised.

A man walked over, obviously concerned seeing Emily and Clarence together. He grabbed her arm and firmly pulled her away. 'Get away,' he demanded. She looked up at the two men towering over her, looking at one and then the other. She tugged on both of their arms and pleaded for them not to argue.

'Daddy, please don't shout.' Both men looked

down at her, seeing her deep blue eyes, and Clarence realised he was looking at Daniel Grayson.

'Daniel Grayson?'

'And who might be asking?' the man answered.

'Detective Chief Inspector Clarence Landon, and Emily's stepfather.'

'I see. Then you have many questions.'

The bustling coffee shop offered a serene and refreshing experience. Classic Italian music played at a mild volume that complemented the coffee-sipping chit chat between Clarence and Daniel. Emily sat in the corner with a colouring book, picking at sweet pancakes and syrup as she scribbled away peacefully. Clarence had so many questions he needed answered, but he wasn't sure whether Daniel wanted to answer them.

'Ava has been arrested,' Clarence admitted.

'For what reason?' Daniel queried.

'For your murder of course.'

'I see.'

'Care to explain?' Landon requested.

'Will you leave me and my daughter alone if I do?'

'That depends on you.'

The truth was Ava *had* caved in Daniel's skull with a skillet. What she hadn't realised was, Daniel was still alive when she buried him.

Coming home late when you're in a relationship with Ava meant Daniel had dug his own grave. Ava had struck him by surprise, and it knocked him unconscious. But he didn't realise he had been hauled into a grave, and buried six feet under. Even to this day, Daniel is surprised he survived. Even the likes of Houdini attempted that escape and very nearly failed. Daniel recalled regaining consciousness just as the first shovel of soil was thrown at him. Each and every shovel weighted his body further into the ground, causing the feeling of someone standing on his chest. Ava hadn't stuck around. If she had, she could have bashed him over the head for a second time and actually done the job properly. Daniel kept thinking, *"I've got to get out of here",* and gave it his best effort. All he could think about was his daughter and imagining her helping him out of the grave. He had blood all over his face, a cracked rib, and bruising, but that was a better outcome than the alternative. In the movies, people are buried alive all the time, and if they don't die they come out unscathed. But that wasn't what Daniel experienced. It's rare anyone even survives such a horrible fate, and those who do often suffer irreparable damage to their bodies. Daniel was still undergoing physical therapy, and he still flinched at trapped nerves caused by overexertion when he kicked and punched his way out of the grave. His mouth and nose filled with dirt, cutting off his air flow, and as his hand broke free through the surface, the dirt was even in his eyes. As he clawed his way out of the grave, spitting out the dirt, he rolled on to his back, and at that moment he had clarity.

Nothing else mattered to Daniel. He momentarily paused the retelling of his story and looked at Emily. She had finished her pancakes and was still quietly colouring in her book. Clarence was also sitting quietly. He didn't dare interrupt Daniel's confession, but he raised his brows to signal permission for Daniel to continue.

As Daniel freed himself from the grave, the dark night engulfed him. He had no idea of his whereabouts, and only when he saw the old tattered shed did he realise where he was. As he began his walk down the dark road, the tarmac was slick from dew. There had been a slight drizzle in the air, and a chill forced him to hunch his shoulders as he held his ribcage. As the wind howled, not a car passed for what felt like eternity. *Will someone recognise me?* He wondered. *Or will I continue down this dark road?* He used all his senses and instincts to find refuge. The road was desolate, street lamps were mere balls of dim light, and the only sound came from a cat slinking through the bushes, but eventually he came across a fuel station.

The road to recovery would be a long and drawn out process. He hated being away from his daughter, but he wasn't prepared to let Ava get away with what she had just tried to do.

Daniel Grayson wasn't a violent man. He made more money than Ava could spend, and his drive to protect and expand Grayson construction was stronger than ever.

Wallace and Claudia Henderson were keeping their heads low in Harlow when Wallace received the phone call from Daniel. It was then Daniel explained to Wallace what had happened and whether Wallace wanted it or not, he was to prove vital in the execution of Daniel's plan. Wallace didn't have a choice. He conned Daniel out of thousands of pounds, and if he wanted to wipe the slate clean, he'd do exactly as Daniel instructed or it was back to jail for more than just conning him out of money. Daniel had the dirt, quite literally.

The first part involved Claudia and Wallace uprooting and moving into the quiet cul-de-sac. Of course, at this moment in time, Wallace hadn't even known about Ava's past, but he was keen to help a friend out, especially one who had been buried alive. That's what he told himself anyway. But when he saw Ava, he laughed it off as a sick joke from Daniel; a bitter ex just wanting custody of his child.

On the evening of Emily's disappearance, Daniel left his car a couple of streets behind the Willows residence, and walked to avoid detection. When he looked down at his watch and saw the time was 9 o'clock, he waited by the local phone box, close to the Henderson's home.

The coast was clear for Daniel to strike. Wallace had removed the house keys from Ava's bag whilst she was in the bathroom and gave them to Daniel by the back door. The two men nodded to one another, and they parted ways. As far as Wallace was concerned, his part had been done.

But the question as to why Daniel went through this elaborate plan still niggled at Clarence.

As Daniel sipped his coffee, he smiled at Clarence. 'What better way to avenge my death than to take the most precious thing she has. Besides, she wouldn't suspect *me* now, would she?'

Emily continued to colour like a snapshot of time. Her blonde tresses blowing from the breeze that wafted in from the door. Her youthful face turned towards Clarence, and she giggled. Under the long blonde fringe shone eyes the colour of the sea itself and a nose as cute as a button; he loved her like his own daughter. But she wasn't. She was Daniel's daughter.

'Promise me, Daniel, that you will cherish that girl with all your heart,' Clarence sobbed.

CHAPTER 30

Truth will prevail

Leaving Emily had been one of the hardest things Clarence had ever had to do, and it was followed by locking up Ava Willows and saying goodbye to that chapter in his life. But he left Harlow knowing Emily was alive and well. That was the right thing to do. Now, he just had to hold his end of the bargain and fulfill a small request by Daniel.

Clarence Landon didn't really know if he could trust his instincts anymore. After all, he got it completely wrong when it came to Ava; the one person who could deceive him. They say those that cry the loudest are not always those that are hurt the most. If people can hurt you, *really* hurt you, then they're generally the ones close enough to do it. As Clarence headed home, he drove and contemplated his future. He looked across at the small package on the passenger seat and wondered if he should make the delivery sooner rather than later.

Revenge wasn't part of Clarence's vocabulary, but he understood the need for payback, a way of settling the score and administering retribution. Daniel's plan took approximately six months to execute, a trivial but consuming task. Clarence had witnessed revenge with often shocking results; affairs being one of the greatest causes of revenge, often involving some sort of criminal activity. But how far was too far, bearing in mind that it can continue in a vengeful cycle. *Before you **seek revenge** with someone be sure and **dig two graves.***

Clarence slowed his driving as the heavens opened. He found it ironic that during the time he spent with Emily there was literally a ray of sunshine, and now as he left, the water sang as it tapped the car roof. With the steady drumming of water droplets on the car's windscreen, the clouds softened and the moon's light brought a comforting beauty to the darkness.

Whilst Clarence understood the reasons behind Daniel's revenge, it wasn't something he himself, would undertake. Clarence believed while revenge might make us feel powerful, it actually turns us into victims; victims of negative thoughts and emotions. Planning personal vindication could easily affect someone's mental health, and in Daniel's case, months from his life. Of course, this case was different, they all are, but an innocent nine year old child got caught in the middle of their feud. This wasn't some Shakespeare play where Othello's vengeful behaviour acts as a catalyst for every event or a youth on the path of vengeance to avenge his father. No, this was about ensuring the safety of Daniel's daughter.

Clarence had visited Broadmoor Hospital only once before, and it was notorious for housing Britain's most violent criminals and was originally built as a criminal lunatic asylum in 1863. Even back then it housed ninety-five female patients, and a block for men followed a year later. When it first opened, in the Victorian age, no drugs or psychological treatment were used as it was intended for the safe custody and treatment of the criminally insane. And it became popular through the years as people enjoyed the regime of rest and the conditions were often better than they had had at home. Unfortunately every patient within the Broadmoor walls had a sad beginning, and most don't end with happy endings. It was common chat at the police station that staff were dealing with patients attacking and torturing one another, and the staff often had to stop obsessive fans when they tried to visit the famous, high profile inmates. Broadmoor housed dozens of sadistic killers, and when staff read about Broadmoor's patients and their gruesome crimes, it left them scared for life. Clarence didn't really know what to expect. On one hand Broadmoor was feared, and on the other it had gangster Bobby Day living a life of luxury with his own butler and tailor. Clarence didn't want to visit Bobby, but it was rumoured he had quite a smart room, decorated with yellows and purples which were very much his colours and so plush it was compared to a hotel. How did a criminal like Bobby Day manage to gain status in the Broadmoor hierarchy and regard himself as being the main man? Eating pork pies and all...

The journey took Clarence approximately an hour and a half to reach Bracknell Forest which was situated at the eastern edge of the village of Crowthorne. It was a beautiful area from what he recalled, and he couldn't fully appreciate its beauty at night.

When he arrived the next day, the site was surrounded by woodland and Edgebarrow Woods. Where the buildings stood at the north-west, they occupied a steep south-facing ridge descending into large terraces that leveled out at the bottom to encompass a garden with surrounding farmland. Clarence approached from the main west drive, west off Crowthorne High Street, and he couldn't really remember where he was going or if he was even headed in the right direction. A sign for "women's range" pointed him to the east at the top of a steep slope, separated from the "men's range" by the approach to the Superintendent's house; a long two-storey brick building that was in-keeping with the style similar to the hospital.

Clarence never really fully understood Burke's term, "If you want to catch a monster sometimes you have to get into bed with them". She always did have an unusual perspective, but he had quite literally been in bed with a monster who found bloodcurdling screams music to her ears.

As he walked into the secure hospital, he was approached by a woman in formal clothing with her hand out-stretched. Clarence looked at her and thought to himself, *she's little.* He felt like picking her up and putting her in a high chair.

'Professor Collins. Are you DCI Landon?'

'I am Clarence Landon, yes, Madam.'

'Superintendent Floyd informed us we were to be expecting you. You're quite the stir of the town. It is a pleasure to meet *the* DCI Landon.'

'Are there others, Madam?' he smiled.

'Did you pay for that ad in the newspaper saying what a clever Detective you are or did they place it themselves?'

'Madam?' Clarence made an unsuccessful attempt to look modest but furrowed his brow at the comment. Looking at her he felt an uncomfortable sensation and sadness crept over him.

'Oh I'm sorry, but you know what newspapers are like nowadays, nothing but smoke. No offence taken, I hope?'

'No,' Clarence grimaced.

'Right then, this way.'

'I'm sorry there must have been a misunderstanding,' he interrupted.

'Don't be shy, Detective, it's not a scene of absolute horror like some depict.'

'That's not quite what I've heard.'

'Well, Detective I would be lying if I said we didn't hold a few patients that have a severe aversion to child molesters. But the incident you may be referring to where serial killer Richard Able murdered fellow inmate John Cummings by torturing him for six hours after locking him in his cell because he was a child molester *is* quite rare. They're just crazy in here.'

'But crazy can describe perfectly the general appearance that, to anyone and everyone, may be ordinary.' Clarence answered.

'Yes...I guess you are right, Mr Landon.' The woman looked towards the floor in angst.

'And yet holding his bloodied corpse up for staff to see through the spy hole is not ordinary!'

'Look, Detective, what happened to Cummings was very unfortunate, and we strive to improve security at all times. I can assure you, you are perfectly safe.'

'I appreciate the invitation, but I must decline. I have allowed enough evil into my heart.' Clarence handed over the small parcel from Daniel – a white envelope unaddressed and unopened.

CHAPTER 31

The most dangerous creation of any society is
those that have nothing to lose.

It had been a time of shocking revelations. Ava had been put away, Clarence felt like the biggest fool going, but Superintendent Floyd and Burke believed it was a happy ending.

The Willows' residence was empty, no child laughing, no clattering of the kitchen utensils as Ava prepared a meal that evening, just silence, and as Clarence opened the fridge door he quietly belched to himself even though he was alone. He apologised for it too. It was just habit. As he waited for the water to boil a knock tapped at the door.

'Clarence, are you in there? Can I come in?' It was Burke. Her voice was flat, it had no intonation. He wondered if he should open the door, but he succumbed to the knocking.

'I've just boiled the kettle. Cup of tea, Tenley?'

'I'd love one, thank you.'

'It seems I'm not the only one, Tenley who is having trouble unwinding,' he huffed.

'It's been a rough time,' she agreed.

'What can I do for you?' he probed as he handed her a mug.

'Thank you,' she said as she sat at the dining room table, eyeing the hole where the knife had penetrated the wood, reminding her of her own tragic past. Tenley ignored Clarence's question at first. Truth was, her house was quiet too, and she just needed some company. She scoped her eyes in awe around the house as she cupped her hands around her mug, and Clarence remained standing watching her.

'Emily's safe and happy!' he stated happily. 'You probably know that already.'

'I did. That's wonderful,' she smiled.

'Are you going to tell me the real reason you're here?'

'Clarence, lighten up. You used to be...'

'Fun?'

'No...not quite the word I was looking for,' she frowned.

'Don't change the subject!' he groaned.

'All right...I want to know how you got on. You know, with Ava,' she sighed.

'I didn't see her.'

'Oh? I thought you had that favour to do.'

'And I fulfilled that favour.'

'God put you on this earth to rid it of crime you know, Clarence. Don't feel guilty. Are you going to drink that or just look at it?' she asked as Clarence eyed his cup.

'It troubles you, doesn't it, Tenley, that the cup in which the tea is poured is perfect in every way, and yet I wait. Please extend your courtesy in giving me some credit where credit is due. I believe you're hiding something.'

'I'm sorry, Clarence. The truth is I'm a little distracted,' she whimpered.

'With the Lawmaker case? If you permit, Tenley, I extend to you my utmost sympathy.'

'For what, Clarence?'

'For whatever ache of the heart you are experiencing.'

'But you do not understand, Clarence...'

'You question why I stay here in this empty house.

I sense the inevitability and yet what can Landon do? Nothing. Like my tea, it sits waiting, waiting for me to drink. Now, are you going to be completely honest with me?'

'I cannot tell you enough how awful these past few weeks have been, Landon.'

'It's all over now,' he reassured her.

'It's a good thing we have you on board.'

'You can always have faith in Landon,' he nodded with a wry smile. 'You know, Burke. I owe the discovery of Emily alive entirely to you,' Clarence smiled.

'Really?' she answered.

'Oh yes, do you remember telling me about the knife?'

'Yes and you zoned out.'

'Mhm...I remembered that Ava used that knife only for special occasions.'

'You don't think...Goodness. But I don't understand why Ava would confess to the murder of Daniel Grayson.'

'Because it is the law that once acquitted, she wouldn't be tried for the same offence twice: once tried, it would be proven that Daniel Grayson hadn't been murdered, and Ava would be safe for the rest of her life.'

'Clever girl.'

'Indeed. I'll never understand women,' he shook his head.

'You have been rather unlucky in love haven't you!'

'What about yourself, Tenley, any men on the horizon?' he sipped.

'No, I'm quite comfortable as a midlife spinster to be honest,' she laughed. 'Perhaps, when we are again together, Burke will explain this thing called love and what it's all about to you,' her eyebrows raised as she smirked.

'Together again?'

'Didn't you hear? Floyd's up for promotion and has reinstated our working relationship to be permanently down here in Sussex. It looks like we're going to be seeing much more of each other.'

'And Operation Lawmaker?'

'About that.....Cheers,' she grinned.

EPILOGUE

Remember me

Dear Clarence,

I have followed with great excitement your commendation of excellence and yet public shame of never finding my daughter Emily. My own shame however, never bothered me apart from the inconvenience of being incarcerated. In our discussions it was apparent that your partner, DI Burke, figures quite highly in your table of values. I think your success in ending one of Sussex's most prolific murderers pleased you because it pleased her.

Do you envision her being shamed by your ignominy? Do you imagine her losing her career because of your indiscretions? What is worst about the events that have unfolded, Clarence? Is it how your failure will reflect on your daddy? God rest his soul.

By the way I noticed my name had been included in the country's most wanted list. You must be very proud of yourself.

Today I woke up in the small bed with lemon coloured sheets, my neck was sore from sleeping on the one pillow and my medicine from the night before had now worn off. I am trapped once again in my insomnia.

My roommate snored and muttered to herself whilst she slept, and I was tempted to shove a pillow over her face for a moment of peace and quiet. The nightmare I had had from the Seroquel induced night came to the surface and reminded me of one of my greatest fears; drowning. I made a mental note to mention it to my psychiatrist later today.

The nurses seemed particularly excited the night before, encouraging me to swallow the antipsychotic drug used for the treatment of Schizophrenia. They claimed, although I may not be Schizo, it was common to use it for other disorders such as Manic Depression or major depression, and also as a sleep aid with its sedating effect and to be taken by mouth. I quite liked how they had to mention that part. They don't call it the funny farm for no reason.

'Good morning, Ava. How are we today?' a nurse asked as she approached the door. Here, time is distinguished by meals and medications. Nothing good came from either, nothing to ever lift my spirits. In here, I have no rights. No freedom. I guess I lost that a long time ago, and I can't choose when I wake or when I sleep. The psychiatrist said I suffer from a borderline personality disorder that manifested itself in tremendous mood swings, slighted where there was no slight and highly suspicious. I didn't give her the satisfaction of an answer, but she didn't seem to care. She smiled at me. 'You have a visitor.'

They labeled it the Seclusion room. A room where the door was never open, there was no light, no handle and certainly no way out; just four concrete walls and a toilet with no paper. Even my orange jumpsuit lacked the ability to hold my attention. I was grateful for anyone and anything. I didn't even know what the time was. Was my visitor coming in five minutes or five hours? Should I try to sleep? Would I even know the difference?

As I sat on the edge of the mattress in the seclusion room, I wished I was back listening to my roommate's snores, and in the silence I heard the distant footsteps approach. They call the place an asylum, but it's anything but. It's a forgotten place where they take your dignity along with your clothing. A small envelope is passed through the letterbox, already opened on the side and I peer through the letterbox hoping to see a glimmer of human life but nothing.

What do you want from me? Do you want me to confess? To cleanse my spirit in the name of Jesus Christ. Admit to the lies that went on through my mouth. Am I what they're calling a multiple killer? I guess so, I've got numbers. All of us have evil inside us, all of us and my evil just happened to come out because of circumstances. So here I am writing down my thoughts, the psychiatrist says it would be therapeutic, but the truth is when I used my knife that was what brought psychological relief. I am Mother Nature's mistake, we all make them. Will you forgive me?

And to break up the day I receive a letter, from a fan no doubt. They've probably kissed it all over, and inside they've declared their love. I can almost feel their glare like a deranged seagull studying a shellfish. I can feel them spreading the hot sauce on me already.

I imagine you sitting alone, bent over, and twiddling your stache while you read this. Am I accurate? Please say so, truly.

Regards your better half.

A.

~

Ava handed over her letter and pen to the warden after signing her initial. As she sat, she withdrew the contents of the envelope she had been handed and a handful of dirt fell to the floor. Her eyes rested without blinking upon the contents and her lips gave away her intention. Her stare was an icy hostility, a powerful hatred with a pensive grimace. She was frozen as she read just two words that were written.

Remember me?

~

ACKNOWLEDGEMENTS

First and foremost, I wish to thank my amazing other half Cliff, thank you for believing in me when I started this venture, when it was all just a dream. Thank you for making it become a reality. To Sue, for being my tough-love advice guru, I'm grateful for your support and friendship and your eagle eyes for those sneaky typos. Also to Andrea, for persevering with me. This book wouldn't be what it is without you both.

To my loyal readers, thank you for following me and enjoying my stories as much as I enjoy writing them. I'd be honoured to continue bringing you more stories from my existing characters and introducing new.

Last but not least, I'd like to thank you! – the person that has just finished reading this book. I hope you enjoyed it and if you didn't, I hope to try harder next time.

If you enjoyed this book, please let the author know by leaving a review on Amazon, and whilst you're there why not check out some of the other books by E.J. Wood. In order of publication

STANDALONES
Beyond The Pale – a psychological thriller
The Forgotten Man – a historical fiction short story
Amalie – a historical serial killer thriller

SERIES
(DCI Landon book 1) The Kidnapper's Word
– a historical suspense

Also from E.J. Wood

A historical serial killer thriller

Read on for an extract from

AMALIE

They murdered families.
The Fuhrer cannot protect them now.

It's not wise to murder the family of a budding assassin. Created by Auschwitz, her skill is honed by revenge.

A very different type of serial killer is loose in 1950s Europe. In Britain, a Brotherhood of powerful men takes notice and enhances the expertise and artistry of a killer.

DCI John Owen was born to serve. Recruited by MI6, he tracks an accomplished executioner whose love of luxury and the arts is second only to the love of watching an early death come to those who truly deserve it.

Join the chase. Then ask yourself...
Can there ever be only one winner?

Available on Amazon

PROLOGUE

BROADMOOR HOSPITAL
The year is 1980

You call me crazy, a monster and many other derogatory names. You see, the authorities see me as a problem they cannot solve. Their easy way out would be to bury me in a concrete coffin; out of sight, out of mind. It doesn't matter to them the reasons behind my actions, they don't know the answers, and they don't really care.

My life in solitary is unbroken depression. My furnishings consist of soft compressed cardboard, I imagine so I don't hurt myself? Or is it for your safety? And my sink and lavatory are bolted to the floor next to a concrete slab as my bed; things haven't improved in the last forty years then?

I'm left to vegetate and regress, but with no one listening what's the point? Isn't the idea of solitary confinement just that? Solitary…

"'To see a world in a grain of sand, and a heaven in a wild flower", and all… Had the English poet William Blake foreseen the cruelties and barbarism against innocents when he wrote Auguries of Innocence back in 1803? Pitting rich against poor, innocent against mature, all opposites to show hypocrisy in contemporary life? Was he a genius or a madman? I'll let you decide.

They put me in this 6ft x 9ft cell with a Perspex wall hoping to learn about me, break me? They say if I behave myself they will give me special privileges;

I've heard THAT one before. Just give me a cyanide tablet and be done with it! Wouldn't that be easily and swiftly resolved, if Amalie Keller just...died?

Entertainment is rather...bleak might I add? Persuading an inmate to swallow her tongue was only light entertainment for what was it... ten minutes? Of course, that was until they moved me here. A DANGER TO SOCIETY...they labelled me. She was doomed when she said, "I don't know what your problem is Keller, but I bet it's hard to pronounce."

I thought it most courteous to say when the warden passed my Perspex window that, "We're going to be one short on roll call today." Dr Harlow didn't see the humour in it; dull bastard.

My feelings towards Dr Harlow grow increasingly with, I'm sure, a mutual hatred, and his lording over me sickens me as he tries to incompetently quantify me.

Broadmoor Hospital is for the criminally insane and those whose sanity is being evaluated. The general administrator, Dr Walter Harlow, is as pompous as they come and an incompetent director for the sanatorium that he has been assigned. His petty punishments don't go unnoticed, and his growing jealousy of my willingness to share information with law enforcement rather infuriates him, but it gives me great pleasure.

His mediocrity and self-importance make my skin crawl. I laughed out loud when I saw him on the four o'clock news boasting about new evidence now that he has a name, "Hansom Tiling," in a cold case for which he so desperately wants credit for solving. That should keep him occupied for a while. But, giving him the name gave me what I wanted, and that was access to the prison library so I can occupy myself with good quality literature. Speaking of that big bald fuck – here he comes now.

'Keller,' Dr Harlow states while standing in front of me.

'Any rational society would let me die,' I answer.

'Why would we do that? You're our most prized asset.' He grimly smiles. 'Besides, you know Capital Punishment was outlawed back in '69.'

'"Do what you will. This world is a fiction and made up of contradiction".'

'Excuse me?' Harlow asked.

'William Blake.'

'Who?' Harlow croaked.

'One of England's greatest poets of all time…. I don't really have all the crayons to explain it to you.' He looked at me with that vacant look, like the lights were on but no one was home. 'We live to die. We wage war to achieve peace. This world is a paradox.'

'Oh, Amalie, cheer up. You're so confined in your delusional thinking that you really cannot see just how monstrous you are.'

'You have no idea.'

'You still think you're going to be sipping Martinis on some beach? I don't think so, somehow. If you've been told otherwise, I'd seriously reconsider who your friends are. Now, stand facing the wall, place your hands on your head, and do not move. Understood?'

'Whatever you say, Doctor.'

'Good. You have a visitor.'

You see, way back then, when I was born, the world was just cops and robbers. Then IT happened and the world was never the same again, and neither was I.

II

HUNGARY

CHAPTER 1

Never forget

It was September, 1939, and so the Second World War began. Germany invaded Poland on the 1st and the USSR on the 17th.

Nine-year-old Amalie stood in the back garden with her brother Jakob. Little did they know this day was the last day before their lives irrevocably changed. Jakob, four years her senior, took Amalie's hand and pulled her towards the garden; a rich field of green velvet surrounded by splashes of red berries, the flower beds a riot of colour and weed-free. The freshly cut grass offered that summertime scent. But summer was over, and although the sun was high, the days were cooler even on days that lacked clouds.

Every day leaned towards the inevitable colder winter ahead with each night's darkness arriving sooner than the night before, and the sun would rise and set as if in a hurry to reach winter.

'Amalie, Amalie,' her brother called. They laughed as they played and she returned his smile.

'A for Amalie,' Jakob explained.

'A…malie,' she answered.

'This way, hurry,' Jakob tugged her arm.

The children giggled as they played. As the golden rays of the morning sun emerged, the birds chirped their melodious choruses, and her brother paused as their parents bellowed for them to come inside.

'Children, breakfast is ready!'

As they paused their play, the children felt the ground shudder. The distant drone of explosions rumbled across the garden, her brother grabbed her hand and they ran back home for safety.

The grass was laid out like a royal carpet with the reds and golds from the sun high above, and the children inhaled the fresh air. The trees swayed gracefully against the light wind, and the autumn breeze carried fine drops with a promise of rain.

As the children entered the yard, their father was panicked.

'Amalie, Jakob, where have you been? Hurry, quickly!'

'Jakob, come here, help me,' their mother called and the children's eyes widened with concern.

'Darling, we must go. Everything is ready, we don't have much time,' their father bellowed as he packed the cart.

'I just need help gathering the rest of my belongings, Leo, please send Jakob! I can't carry it all.'

'Jakob, help your mother, but hurry.'

Amalie climbed into the wagon as the Keller family prepared to leave everything behind, and Jakob ran upstairs to gather the rest of their belongings. As the wagon headed West, Amalie thought about the conversations she and her brother Jakob had heard; they overheard their parents discussing the rise of Nazism and the possibility of evacuation. Of course, at the time they didn't understand. Germany quickly became transformed into a totalitarian state, and nearly all aspects of life became controlled by the government. When the national referendum of 1934 confirmed Hitler as a sole leader, his word became the highest law, and racism, especially anti-Semitism, became a central ideological feature.

Amalie knew big changes were happening. Her father was home more, their food rations were much smaller, and their mother cried almost every day. Education suffered, their school was damaged by bombing, and the next nearest school had been requisitioned by the government. Young male teachers were called to fight the war, and the students were asked to help raise money for knitting comforters for the troops, a talent her mother had passed on to her.

Adolf Hitler had been a name frequently mentioned and as his Party rose in popularity, the hatred for the Jewish people increased; blaming them for the problems of Germany. Although Amalie's father was British born, her mother was Jewish, and as the hatred grew with the country's poor economic crisis, the family was forced to leave their home and everything they had come to love.

'We're moving away so we will be safe, the fighting won't be near us.' Leo whispered to the children.

Amalie's mother stroked the girl's hair.

'Don't worry, darling, it's just an adventure,' she said. 'Don't be afraid.'

The journey to Belgium was long and tiresome. As the Kellers travelled through the sylvan areas, the wind howled and blew a bitter chill. The leaves danced among the white blanket of velvet snow beneath them, and the smell of woodland decomposition and tall silhouettes offered no reassurance that the Kellers were doing the right thing; fleeing their home for a haven in a non-Nazi controlled part of Europe. As eyes all around watched them travel, it was obvious they were just as vulnerable here as when they were home, and an unnerving presence of evil lurked as if the Devil himself was waiting for the Kellers to make a mistake before he made his move and they became prey to the forest.

Living as refugees in Belgium, their father smiled more, her mother stopped crying, and Jakob and Amalie went back to school. She learned the language, made new friends, they had a new home, and life was great.

'Amalie,' Jakob smiled and attracted Amalie's attention whilst she bathed in a tin bath from the water they had heated from the large copper near the fire. Bath day was once a week, and it was this day their mother also baked fresh bread. At this point, the SS were exterminating their friends, those they left behind. People who couldn't leave with them were presumed murdered; the Germans weren't far away when their father ordered them to leave. As night-time fell, their stomachs rumbled, Father and Jakob went looking for food; the forest once plentiful of game is now quiet. The winter has moved all the animals away so they return empty-handed. Their mother prepared some vegetables she salvaged from home, but their portions were small, and Amalie noticed that her mother went without.

'We can't continue like this, Leo.' Eva whispered to her husband, hugging him close to her chest.

'I know.'

On the 10th of May, 1940, the Nazis invaded Belgium. New laws and regulations were introduced.

First came the soldiers and then came the men in black, the SS. There were loudspeakers, with speeches declaring loud and clear what they wanted.

Amalie wasn't allowed outside; they couldn't go out, watch a movie, or see friends. Her father lost his job, and they had to change schools again. The Kellers missed their old home. Here they had an outside lavatory and no bathroom to wash in. The daughter shared a bed with her brother next to their parents, and their food once again had been rationed. What food Leo could barter for, such as meat, butter, eggs, and cheese were less bountiful, and their mother tried harder to grow their own vegetables.

The air had a cold malevolent tone to it, the wind howled and explosions offered a never-ending moan. As the night fell, a dense fog rolled, lights flickered from across the field holding them in fear. They clung to each other tightly and quivered, waiting for the bullets to slaughter them like sheep.

The hairs on Amalie's neck rose like pins with the terror of it all.

'Amalie,' her brother took her hand and squeezed it, gently offering comfort.

Terror had sucked every breath from her mouth and she was unable to answer.

'It's a tank, it's the Russians!'

'Under the table,' her father shouted.

'EVERYBODY OUT!' The soldier demanded, 'Are you, Roma?'

'No.' Leo answered hugging his wife tightly and signalling the children to be quiet.

'Are you Jews?' the soldier asked.

'Yes.' Eva proudly answered.

'Eva, no,' Leo grabbed her tightly.

'It's OK. They're not here for us....are you?' she looked over.

'The children can stay in the house, we just want supplies,' the soldier nodded and smiled.

The Keller parents stood to the side, and Amalie cried out to her mother, 'Mother,' and Jakob yelled to father, 'Papa' as the Luftwaffe unleashed its reign of terror. The Russians retaliated and the Kellers ran for cover.

'Mama!' Amalie screamed. As Leo and Eva ran for cover, the world around them felt like hell on earth. The Luftwaffe flew low and unleashed their hail of death on the unsuspecting Soviets. A fire broke out and clouds of smoke surrounded the Kellers, suffocating them. As soon as the bombs dropped, the world as Amalie had known it became a luminescent fireball. Thick grey ash billowed into the sky, and they became shrouded by a veil of dark smoke. The fire flicked and crackled and crawled up the trunks of the surrounding trees, enveloping them whole. It devoured everything in its path, and its intense heat forced the family outside their home.

'Papa,' Jakob yelled out but to no answer. The painful silence and all the nerves in the children's bodies pleaded for the catastrophe to stop.

'AMALIE, JAKOB, LEO?' Eva cried out and ran towards the children, rushing them inside away from the chaos. Her voice quivered in overwhelming fear as she searched for her husband.

Leo stormed open the door, shoving it closed behind him, and the Luftwaffe disappeared from view. He could feel death swallowing him whole, and he raised a finger to his lips to silence the other members so he could listen for the aircraft to encircle.

CHAPTER 2

"Surviving is the only glory in war."
Samuel Fuller

Amalie wrote to her Grandparents in Britain often, her Nan lived for her granddaughter's letters. She missed the grandchildren dearly, and every day she would wait at the entrance of her home for the postman to bring her another letter. Never did they mention the horrors the Keller children were experiencing, instead Amalie was brief and buoyant. Her grandparents were old and frail, and they needn't know about the atrocities where the Kellers resided. Over the next few days, Amalie started to miss her grandparents; she wrote them the letter in hopes of seeing them once again.

Hi Nana,

I am in the best of health and it's my birthday tomorrow. I wish you were here. For the moment, my lessons have been suspended, there are many changes here. Well, things are moving pretty smoothly, all I do is eat and sleep, if I don't get out soon I will look like a barrel. I'd like to buy a dress for my birthday but every day Mother is crying and I don't know why. I try to comfort her but it doesn't help. Father is sad and says I cannot have the new dress. He says I will have to wait until the war is over. It is very boring here and we're always hungry. When can I see you again?

She never did recall whatever happened to that letter, and she never did see her nana again.

Amalie's mother and father came home one

evening wearing a badge on their clothing and pinned two more on the coats of their son and daughter. Amalie looked straight into her mother's blue eyes, once bright and ambitious now grey and dead.

'Amalie, come here please, lift your arm.' Leo instructed his daughter to raise her arm so the yellow star could be attached to her clothing. A yellow star with "Jude" ("Jew") inscribed in the centre of the patch. This badge made a distinction; the previous day just a person on the street but now, there were Jews and non-Jews.

'This is ludicrous.' Eva shook her head at Leo whilst she stitched the badge onto the clothing.

'We don't have any choice.' Leo waved a poster he snatched from the wall outside. It read, *"Remember the badge, have you already put on the badge? Before leaving the building, put on the badge!"*

'Everyone is staring, Leo, we can't carry on like this. We're like prisoners in our own home.'

The badge represented more than humiliation, it meant shame. It meant fear. If the Kellers forgot their badge, they faced being fined, imprisoned, or worse. Families had been beaten and put to death as a constant reminder not to forget their badges.

Eva ceased smiling. She became void. Her eyes were dazed, and her confidence disappeared, isolating herself in a room. She became a shadow of her old self. The shine in her eyes never returned, and she gave up. Amalie's friend, Beatrice Muchmann, had said, "Having to wear the yellow star was the moment when deep fear and misery took hold."

By now Amalie was salvaging scrap metal, paper, wasted food, and glass for recycling. Despite the sadness, she played with other children. Bomb sites were tempting play areas, and she found many gems among the rubble, finding shrapnel souvenirs and chippings of broken pottery. The American servicemen were very generous; she remembered one giving her chewing gum and chocolate, something her parents could never afford. She and her brother often ran off to parties held by the servicemen at their bases; one advised Amalie to always have her eyes on the sky.

By June, 1940, small scale bombing raids began on Britain, and so the Battle of Britain began. Concerned for his parents, Mr Keller placed his wife and children in hiding.

'You can't leave us now!' Eva pleaded with her husband.

'Keep your heads low, stay out of trouble. I will be back as soon as I can. But, I just can't leave Ma and Pa on their own.'

'Father,' Amalie cried. Her father bent down to kiss his daughter and cupped her face into his hands.

'Amalie, I'm going to check on Nana and Grandpa. I won't be long.'

Jakob cuddled Amalie close and nodded at his father.

'Take care of the girls for me, Jakob; you're the man of the house while I'm away.'

'Yes, Papa.'

Leo pulled his coat up towards his face and grabbed his case; he left at dusk and returned to Britain. The Kellers never saw him again.

Many Jews concealed their identity and continued to live with false identification; others hid in attics and shelters. For the Kellers, hiding was a task that took an extraordinary risk. Their mother took them to many shelters, but they were full. The family couldn't stay where they were or they would starve. They were forced closer and closer to the city.

'Please take us,' she cried to the shelter.

'Two children, that is all,' the woman answered.

'I beg you.'

Amalie looked at her mother pleading and tugged at the shelter lady. 'Please, our daddy has already gone.'

'OK fine, but there is not enough food as it is.'

'I won't eat,' her mother answered, relieved.

She cried more this day, hugging the children tightly, wiping their faces and kissing their cheeks.

'Everything will be OK,' she whimpered.

This summer, the Kellers were ordered to report to the nearby city for deportation, but they stayed at the shelter. They slept and prayed, ate bread and shared the water that was given to them by the non-Jewish family that took them in.

The non-Jewish family explained to the Kellers that life dictated by the Nazi Regime was strange for them as well, and that at a moment's notice the Kellers must go into hiding. Hitler's private army would regularly visit the farm, measure the land and they were the ones who dictated what crops would and wouldn't be needed to be grown. They would count their chickens, dictate how many eggs were to be supplied, and if there were any shortfalls on the quota, then the father would need to purchase them from the Black Market.

The families in hiding were sad, and their ears deafened with the bombings above ground. The shelter had been raided before, the dogs sniffed and sniffed, and they waited motionless, frozen in fear for hours on end, living through hours of terror, but this day was different.

The hatch opened, and the man shouted.

'You must go, NOW.'

But it was too late; the police had found their hiding place.

'There you are, little rats,' an SS smiled.

'How could you?' cried the shelter lady to the farmer.

'I had no choice,' he mouthed.

'And you will be rewarded for your loyalty.' The soldier turned to the farmer and flicked him a gold coin. Catching it greedily, the farmer left and the SS pulled the families out from the shelter by their hair. The dogs barked and snarled, their teeth glistening in the moonlight pushing the prisoners closer together like sheep. The screams were loud as a blood-curdling scream could be, and the Kellers were loaded onto transport like cattle.

'What is happening?' Eva cried out to the other families. She was distraught, grabbing at the clothing of the fellow Jews that are pushed and shoved onto the wagons. 'Where are we going?'

'Shush, stay quiet or you will get us all killed.' A woman angrily snarled.

'Get moving,' a uniformed man snapped and pushed the butt of his rifle at the nape of Eva's neck.

'Auschwitz,' whimpered a man huddled in the corner of the wagon from a previous pickup.

The families were loaded and prepared for their journey to Auschwitz-Birkenau; a concentration and extermination camp. Each transport consisted of one thousand people, a mixture of men, women, and children of all different ages all squeezed into wagons like cattle. Jakob spoke loudly among the chaos; he tried to calm the storm.

'Please everyone stay calm.'

'Shut up, little boy.'

'Please! You're frightening the children. Please just sit where you can.'

He tried to calm the terror and sought order by asking that half of the young people stand and the other half sit, taking it in turns to alternate every four hours whilst the older people, women and children, would be permanently seated to make this three-day journey as comfortable as possible. Some of the carts were open-topped, others were closed. A bucket was tossed inside for human waste, and once the last prisoner was loaded, there was a muffled sound of closing bolts. A whistle blew and the train started moving. The doors were shut, leaving them in almost complete darkness, and the grills were closed to prevent escape. A flicker of light and air filtered through the cracks. This was a journey that some didn't survive; and a journey that Amalie would never forget; there was no food, no water and people collapsed from exhaustion.

'My baby is dead, my baby is dead!' one woman shouted hysterically and the Kellers could do nothing to comfort her. Amalie wanted to jump but God forbid they landed in Germany. The cart remained quiet for most of the journey, a few stops with the soldiers yelling, 'If anyone is missing you will be punished,' whilst pointing the rifle in the prisoner's direction.

The soldiers poked and prodded the prisoners, they laughed among themselves. 'Let's throw them off.'

People wanted to survive; it was a dog-eat-dog time and everyone panicked if someone tried to escape through the small window on the side of the wagon, and Amalie, too, was frightened the SS would shoot if they escaped.

She stayed where she was, her face looking outward from the slats of the wooden wagon. The breeze offered slithers of fresh air that kept the nauseating stench at bay. As the bodies pushed and shoved, tempers rose. Her brother grabbed her pulling her close to his body, and he whispered calmly into her ear.

'I'll protect you, for as long as I shall live.'

By the time they arrived at their destination, four people had already died.

They were shuffled off the wagon into queues staying with their mother and some other two thousand people, and they reached out urgently among the swarm and confusion. Possessions were eagerly snatched away and put to one side, and the people were shoved to the other side.

People were crying, dogs were barking, everyone tried to make sense of this place; a place they never knew existed. The large German Shepherd dogs barked, and their coats were covered in mud. As they growled at the prisoners, their mouths salivated with hunger. Their teeth were sharp and visible as they glared with a wild craze at the frightened people. The dogs' paws scraped at the ground whilst they tugged at the leads. They were monsters.

The children were holding onto their mother for dear life, and prisoners who knew their fate whispered warnings to the newcomers.

'Don't say you're too young, don't say you're ill. Say you are fit and healthy, strong and you want to work and don't say you belong together.'

'Put on my coat, Amalie, so you look bigger,' her mother whispered.

'No Mother, I don't need it.'

'Just do it! Listen to me for once.'

Amalie prepared herself to be older but the SS-man did not ask any questions. A Nazi guard looked at Amalie and hesitated but motioned with a stick. Jakob and Amalie were to be pulled to the left and their mother was pulled to the right. There was no time for goodbyes. Jakob and Amalie were left holding onto each other, Amalie cried for her mother.

'Mother? Where is my mother going?'

At this moment, Amalie hadn't realised it would be the last time she would ever see her mother's face; it would be the last memory of her, screaming as she was dragged away from her children.

A woman standing beside Amalie and Jakob pointed to a smoking chimney. 'There, that is where she's going.'

They were herded into a hall to undress, thankfully away from the sun that burned their skin.

After registration, the children were stripped of clothing and prepared for their hair to be shaved. For the first time, Amalie felt inhuman, stripped of any identity. She looked around and saw many other girls her own age with clippers cutting each other's hair. Tears descend her cheeks as her brown locks fell to the ground.

'Now we all look alike,' a girl said to her. 'Doesn't matter if you are rich or poor, blonde or brown-haired, we will all share the same fate.'

Jakob wore a striped uniform, a size too small, and a striped cap. As the cold metal blade of the scissors touched Amalie's skin she winced and for the first time, she saw her brother cry. But allowing the humiliation of having her head shaved enabled Amalie to pass the first test.

Before dawn, the prisoners were roused from their

overcrowded wooden beds for roll call.

It was their early wake-up call. The prisoners were addressed in German, and a girl next to Amalie kindly translated as a new crowd of Jews were escorted into the camp. They queued up alongside Amalie's group and she overheard the conversation.

'WILLKOMMEN IN AUSCHWITZ.'

'He's welcoming us to Auschwitz,' she whispered.

'QUIET! "I am Franz Hössler. I am in charge of the economic function of the camp, and on behalf of the camp administration, I bid you welcome. This is not a holiday resort but a labour camp. Just as our soldiers risk their lives at the front to gain victory for the Third Reich, you will have to work here for the welfare of a new Europe. How you tackle this task is entirely up to you. The chance is there for every one of you. We shall look after your health, and we shall also offer you well-paid work. After the war, we shall assess everyone according to his merits and treat him accordingly. Now, would you please all get undressed? Hang your clothes on the hooks we have provided and please remember your number. When you've had your bath, there will be a bowl of soup and coffee or tea for all. Oh yes, before I forget, after your bath, please have ready your certificates, diplomas, school reports, and any other documents so that we can employ everybody according to his or her training and ability."'

'He says we are in a labour camp, but he's lying to them. Those poor unsuspecting souls have no idea what lies before them in those chambers.'

Amalie laughed explosively full of shock and horror.

'We arrived and saw the smoking chimneys. But, this is a factory isn't it?' Amalie's mouth dropped open as the other prisoners enlightened her to the harsh reality; the smoke that rose was from the crematorium.

'We must warn them!' Amalie pleaded.

'Then you will die, there is nothing we can do for them.'

The entire camp stood in their meagre clothing and was rushed into queues so their names could be called, standing completely still for hours at a time. Come sunshine or rain, orders and instructions were read out as everyone was counted. Jakob stood next to his sister and cupped Amalie's bare scalp, it was all the comfort he could offer. She closed her eyes and folded her arms tightly around herself and she reminded herself of the words:

ARBEIT MACHT FREI
WORK SETS YOU FREE

It had offered Amalie the false hope that hard work would result in her and her brother's freedom.

As many as nearly two thousand prisoners at a time would have to share the toilet facilities, and the smell was eye-watering. It was a concrete block with a hole to sit on. Only in 1944 were sinks and toilets installed in a small area for each block. They had no sanitation or privacy, and men, women, and children would share, having to wash in dirty water. No soap and no change of clothing for months on end. Within a few days, her brother's once small uniform began to hang. After they were counted, they waited patiently, not uttering a word, waiting for their bowl of soup. Amalie was lucky if she found a potato peel, and the accompanying piece of black bread allowed for slightly better digestion of the watery soup.

'Make it last,' an inmate advised, but she was so hungry. Food played a huge role at the camp and was also one of the greatest problems. The rations were merely to keep them alive but not enough for nutrition or energy that they needed. Many died during the night, so she stole their bread they had saved. She mumbled to herself, 'and I'm taking your boots, too.' Every day was taken as it came. She smuggled fruit into her trousers and potatoes she put into her clogs. First, they took the young, then the older ones, then the parents. They wanted to annihilate them. When the children had to report to work, she begged her brother not to go but he had no choice. They knew they had to work, if they worked they were safe because they were profitable. Without work, the prospect of surviving was slim.

'Nothing leaves this house,' a guard spewed. The female SS in charge was the cruellest person Amalie had ever seen. She barked at the prisoners, kicked and pulled at their ears to hurry along and she remembered her name as if it was inscribed on her arm like the tattoo they were given.

One male guard had decided Amalie didn't resemble a Jew; he was much kinder, treated her nicer and gave her food.

As she would fall asleep she would dream, she would dream that she would be reunited with her mother and father and this was all just a horrific nightmare. Amalie woke from the stench, nervous, hysterical and covered in sweat, to the rotting smell of bodies decomposing outside her confinement. The flies circling indicated they had been there for a while but still she had hope, as long as the sun shined it was a new day and as the light beamed onto her face she realised she would survive. She prayed she wouldn't die after her mother, but she couldn't face being alone either.

Sharing the bed with her brother made the impossible just about bearable. With very little to eat and one blanket to share, starvation rations, disease, lice and bed bugs, all that mattered was that they were together and it was what kept her alive. She grabbed her throat and stroked where she could still feel the hands of her father choking her to quell her crying and ironically for a moment she was there again feeling her father's hands around her throat.

~

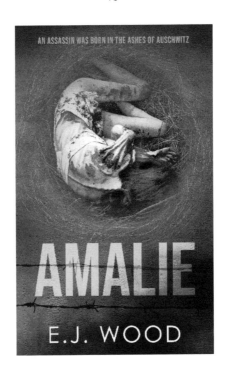

BIBLIOGRAPHY THE KIDNAPPER'S WORD

A Brief History of Scotland Yard | History | Smithsonian Magazine

From the archive, 4 May 1970: Missing children: Parents turn to Scotland Yard | Children | The Guardian

What It's Like To Be Buried Alive — And Survive, September 19, 20155:24 PM ET

Dunning Hayley, HD, A history of burial in London | Natural History Museum (nhm.ac.uk)

PEDOGATE: THE CIA RUNS THE PEDOPHILE RINGS | SOTN: Alternative News, Analysis & Commentary (stateofthenation.co)

Nina Conti & Monkey in Therapy.

Murder of Roy Tutill – Wikipedia

Printed in Great Britain
by Amazon

19687554R00114